THE WITCHING HOURS

BOOK FOUR

BOOKS IN
THE WITCHING HOURS SERIES

THE VAMPIRE KNIFE

THE TROLL HEART

THE GENIE RINGS

THE MERMAID WRECK

THE DRAGON CROWN

THE GIANT KEY
(coming soon)

THE MERMAID WRECK

JACK HENSELEIT

ART BY RYAN ANDREWS

Hardie Grant

CHILDREN'S PUBLISHING

The Mermaid Wreck
first published in 2019
this edition published in 2020 by
Hardie Grant Children's Publishing
Ground Floor, Building 1, 658 Church Street
Richmond, Victoria 3121, Australia
www.hardiegrantchildrenspublishing.com

A catalogue record for this
book is available from the
National Library of Australia

Illustration by Ryan Andrews
Design by Kristy Lund-White

Hardie Grant acknowledges the Traditional Owners of the country on which we
work, the Wurundjeri people of the Kulin nation and the Gadigal people of the Eora
nation, and recognises their continuing connection to the land, waters and culture.
We pay our respects to their Elders past, present and emerging.

Printed in Australia by Griffin Press, part of Ovato, an Accredited
ISO AS/NZS 14001 Environmental Management System printer.

9 10 8

The paper this book is printed on is certified against the
Forest Stewardship Council® Standards. Griffin Press holds
FSC® chain of custody certification SGS-COC-005088. FSC®
promotes environmentally responsible, socially beneficial
and economically viable management of the world's forests.

For Peter, Danny, Jacqueline and Shane
— *and for Beryl, the meanest witch in Australia.*

1

THE BIRTHDAY PARTY

'SHINE THE LIGHT PROPERLY,' SAID MAX. 'I CAN'T see where I'm going.'

Anna rolled her eyes as she pointed her torch towards the ground. The path over the hills was gloomy and wet, but it still wasn't dark enough to complain about. She kicked her foot through a puddle in protest, launching a spray of dirty water at the back of Max's trousers.

Max spun around at once, his eyes fierce. 'Dad!' he said. 'Anna's splashing mud on me!'

Anna stared at him coolly. 'It was an accident.'

Max scowled. 'Dad!' he yelled. '*Dad!*'

He looked around to see if he'd been heard. The Professor was standing wearily at the top of the hill, a suitcase tucked under each arm. He was blinking up at the early twilight stars, a look of polite bafflement on his face. He did not appear to have noticed Max at all.

'Well, I know you did it on purpose,' said Max, turning back to Anna. 'So you'd better not do it again, or I'll –'

'Or you'll do what?' said Anna, narrowing her eyes. 'Go and blab all our secrets? Run off and betray me, *again?*'

Max's cheeks flushed. He marched up the hill without another word, stomping in every puddle he passed. Anna watched him go, her eyes cold.

It was a damp and drizzly evening in Australia. The western sky was rich with colour, still dressed in sunset finery. A cool ocean wind rustled through the spinifex, carrying in the news of the sea.

Anna hefted her rucksack, groaning as the straps cut into her shoulder. A beach holiday in Australia had sounded like a wonderful idea when the Professor first suggested it – a good chance to unwind after all she and Max had been through on their past few trips. But that was before she'd seen the weather forecast. That was before the Professor had got the car bogged on some long-forgotten trail, forcing them to hike the last leg of the journey.

That was before Max's ninth birthday party.

The party, which had taken place just a few days ago, had not started well. The Professor, who had never been very good at planning events, had somehow managed to hire a mime artist instead of a clown, and so the children had spent the first half

3

of the afternoon being creeped out by a strange man who always seemed to be trapped in a box. Max's friends had quickly grown restless, and had decided to explore the house instead – including Anna's bedroom. To her absolute horror, Anna had discovered two of the boys just as they were about to unzip her freshly packed luggage.

'Get away from there!' she had screamed. The boys had fled at once, laughing, but Anna's blood had been pumping so loudly in her ears that she'd barely heard them. Didn't Max know to keep a close eye on his friends while they were in the house? Didn't he remember how important it was to keep their treasures a closely guarded secret? Anna had swiftly checked the bag herself, anxious to ensure all of her artefacts were still inside. *The white knife. The stone heart. The shifting coin.* Her pulse had begun to calm as her fingers brushed against each one.

And then Max's voice had come booming down the hall.

'Look, everybody, look! This is my magic carpet. My *real* magic carpet!'

Anna's heart had almost stopped altogether. She had raced out of her room and into Max's, bursting through the gaggle of schoolboys gathered at his door. She had found Max standing on a piece of carpet that shimmered in shades of blue and silver, his nose stuck proudly in the air. Clutched in his hand was an English-Persian dictionary.

Anna hadn't given him a chance to speak. She had knocked the dictionary from Max's hand and shoved him off the carpet as hard as she could. Then she had chased his friends back through the door, slamming it in their faces.

She had caused such a commotion that the Professor had come running from his study. Max and his friends had been banished to the garden, and Anna had been sent to bed without any cake.

She had barely spoken a word to Max since.

Tears stung at Anna's eyes as she glared down at the muddy track. On each of the Professor's past three work trips, she and Max had seen things so weird and so wild that she could barely believe they had happened at all. They had fought a vampire in Romania with their sneaky friend Isabella, battled a troll in England with their birdwatching friend Jamie, and even outsmarted a witch in Iran with their mischievous friend Caspar, who also happened to be a genie. Anna always remembered her friends fondly, even if their adventures together had sometimes felt more like horrifying ordeals. However, despite all the weirdness of the fabled 'old wood', one rule had always been clear: they could not tell anyone else about the fairy world. Talking about it to anyone else was the most dangerous, stupid and irresponsible thing they could do, for it would risk drawing the fairies' attention to that person as well. Anna knew she and Max had been lucky – more than lucky – to have survived all of their fairy encounters so far. If a monster came calling in their hometown while they were away, Max's snivelling school friends wouldn't stand a chance.

Anna sighed, staring up at the clouds. She had been so lost in her thoughts that she hadn't noticed how much the sky had darkened. Max and the Professor were out of sight. Worse still, her torch had begun to flicker. Anna slapped it, trying to shake the batteries into place.

'Hello?' she called. 'Professor?'

There was no reply. Anna quickened her pace, glancing around at the hilltops. A new shape had appeared in the distance, its silhouette barely visible against the dusky sky: a lighthouse, tall and unlit. Did that mean a town was nearby? Anna hurried along the path.

'Professor?' she called again. 'Hey, Professor!'

A flash of lightning burst through the storm clouds. Anna rose up on her toes, hoping to spot the Professor over the crest of the hill; but in that short moment, all she managed to look at was the lighthouse. The building had dirty white walls and a pointed red roof, and there was a lone tree grow-ing beside it, with scraggly branches and a bushy top. And under the tree, there was …

Anna's heart began to thump in her chest. A person had been standing under the tree – a tall, thin man, dressed all in grey. She squinted into the darkness, crouching a little lower to the ground. The man had been very still, as if he hadn't meant to be seen. What was he doing out so late, standing in the rain? Was he spying on her? Had he come to steal her knife?

And then, without meaning to, Anna laughed. She was being paranoid. The man could be anybody: a holidaymaker admiring the lightning on the horizon, perhaps, or even the lighthouse keeper himself, stepping outside to take the air. The Professor wouldn't be far away. Even Max would be nearby, scrunching up his face at some stupid thought.

This was not an adventure. Anna grabbed the straps of her rucksack as she ran up the hill, splashing her way through a long, deep puddle. Beach grass tugged at her ankles as she crossed the summit, scratching at her skin, dampening her socks –

And then something pulled at her feet, *hard*, and Anna's legs were swept out from under her, and then she was falling down the hill, her torch rolling away, her elbows bruising, her face sliding through mud. She came to an undignified rest at the bottom of the slope, wiping the muck from her eyes in disgust, glaring all around her. *Max*. He had waited at the top of the hill to trip her – she was sure of it.

Where was he hiding now? Anna tried to stand up — and immediately fell over again. Something sticky was wrapped around her ankles, binding her legs together. Anna wriggled onto her side, breaking her feet apart with a mighty kick.

And then Anna heard a noise. It was a small, soft noise, barely louder than the rustling grass, like the hiss of a can being opened, or a bag of knucklebones rattling in the wind — but although she listened closely, she could not work out which direction it had come from. Was *this* something to worry about, or was she being paranoid again? Anna snatched up her torch and shone it towards the hillside, bracing herself for what she might see.

The light fell feebly on the grass. Rain-soaked tussocks swayed back and forth in the salty breeze. But there was nothing else there. The hill was empty.

Unless ...

Anna slowly climbed to her feet. The side of the

hill was slick with shadows, but there was one big patch that looked blacker than the rest – a *very* big patch, just beyond the reach of her torchlight. It was so close that Anna would only need to take a single step off the path before she could see what it was.

Maybe she was being paranoid – but maybe she wasn't. Anna wiped the rain from her face, drawing in a slow, calming breath. She squeezed the torch. She raised her foot.

And then her light went out.

Anna squealed, frantically shaking the torch. The hissing sound was rustling out of the grass again, chirping and clacking, like an orchestra of crickets gone mad. The shadows around her were growing blacker and blacker. Suddenly the sky seemed darker than ever before.

Whatever this was, it definitely wasn't human.

'Stay away,' said Anna, working hard to keep her voice steady. 'I'll hurt you if I have to. I mean it.'

The chittering stopped. Anna gritted her teeth, desperately wishing she could see in the dark. Her fingers twitched.

Something hairy brushed against her forehead.

Anna threw her torch as hard as she could. She heard it strike something in the dark – heard a hiss of displeasure – saw the great shadow recoil – and then she was running as fast as her legs could carry her, splattering her way along the muddy path. But where was she going? Where could she hide? Anna slipped through a puddle, cold water splashing into her shoes. She could see more buildings in the distance now, roofs glinting silver in the moonlight, but the buildings were too far away to reach in time. Should she turn and fight? After all, she did have a weapon: the impossibly sharp white knife she had found in Transylvania was sheathed at her side, ready to be drawn. But how could she fight an enemy she couldn't see?

She was running as fast as her legs could carry her.

'Stay back,' Anna gasped, twisting her head as she ran. 'I'm warning you –'

'Warning me of what?'

Anna yelped. She spun back around, hands stretched out in front of her – and then something was swinging through the air, smacking painfully against her legs. Anna gasped as she tumbled to the ground, staring up in shock at the stranger who had appeared on the path, shrieking in horror as his gnarled hand reached towards her neck.

2

THE MAYOR OF
GHOST TOWN

'GET OFF ME!' SCREAMED ANNA.

The hand recoiled at once. Anna leapt to her feet, reaching for the hilt of the white knife – but the stranger moved faster. A new torch blazed into life, casting light onto an old, craggy face.

'Who are you?' said the stranger roughly. 'What are you doing out here?'

Anna stared up at the man, panting. The stranger

was burly and broad-shouldered, but his body was shaking, his right hand clutching a wooden walking stick. He was wearing a blue woollen jumper, and the hair plastered over his ears was long and snowy white. Anna realised that the man didn't really look threatening at all.

'Who are you?' the man repeated. He waved the walking stick in Anna's general direction. 'What were you thinking, charging down the path like that?'

Anna blinked in confusion. Hadn't the man heard the awful sound? She paused to listen, casting a wary eye over the hillside – but the sound was gone. Anna ran a nervous finger across her forehead, scared to touch the spot where the *thing* had brushed against her. There didn't seem to be anything there.

'Answer me!' said the stranger. 'Are you alone? Are you lost?'

'No, I'm not alone,' said Anna. 'And I'm only a bit lost. My family are up ahead.' She glared at the man in the blue jumper. 'Who are you, then? Why didn't you have your light on before?'

She pointed at the torch. The man tilted his head towards the light, his old face crinkled in surprise. The walking stick wobbled in his hand.

'Ach,' he said. 'Only a child, are you? And here I am, swinging my stick at an innocent young lass.' He forced a smile. 'I'm sorry for hitting you, girl. Archie Silcock's the name. I live around the bay, but I'm the caretaker of this place, so to speak. The only permanent resident you'll find for miles.' He stooped forward into an awkward little bow.

Anna frowned. 'You can't be the *only* permanent resident,' she said suspiciously. 'There's a whole town up ahead. I can see it.'

She shivered as a gust of rain blew down, but Archie didn't even flinch. Anna grabbed the hilt of the knife in alarm as he spun around suddenly, pointing a crooked finger at the moonlit rooftops across the hill.

'A town, you say?' he said. 'Ach, there's not many left who'd call it a town today. That's a ghost town, girl, make no mistake. It's a long and lonely road that must have led you here, now that her name's been scrubbed from all the maps. Ain't s'posed to be no-one out here tonight, 'cept for some daft professor on a research trip.'

A ghost town. Anna let out a groan she didn't even know she'd been holding. The Professor had mentioned a ghost town, but he hadn't told her they'd be staying there. Of course he had forgotten that detail. Of course he had abandoned her on the hills, leaving her to deal with crazy Archie Silcock by herself. Anna rolled her eyes, feeling a funny mixture of exasperation and affection. Why would she have ever expected anything else?

'That professor is my father,' she said wearily. 'I'm his daughter, Anna. My brother, Max, is here too.' She shivered again. 'I guess tonight this place won't be such a ghost town after all.'

Archie grunted. 'The professor's daughter!' he said. 'Ach, I should have known. I'm here tonight to welcome you in – hand over the keys to the city, and all that. The mayor of ghost town, that's me.' He sniffed loudly, tilting his head towards the clouds. 'We'd best be getting on. Don't want to be caught out in a gale, that's for sure. You can take my torch and lead the way, if you like. That light ain't no good to me.'

He held out the torch. Anna cautiously took it from him, unsure of what he meant. Who wouldn't want to use a light in the evening? She flashed the torch at Archie, keen to get a proper look at his face. With a twinge of shock, she saw that his eyes were as white as the moon.

'Aye,' said Archie stiffly. 'Old blind Archie, that's me. No need to be scared, girl. I know these hills like the back of my hand, and the beaches better still. I can get us where we need to go.'

Anna quickly shone the torch at the ground. Now it all made sense. Archie didn't need a light to see because he couldn't see at all. What a surprise he must have got, hearing her running and screaming down the hill! Anna wished she hadn't given the old man such a fright. She didn't feel good about walking into a ghost town in the dark, but it certainly felt better to be doing it with someone by her side. She smiled tentatively at Archie, even though she knew he couldn't see it. The man's expression remained gruff.

'Lead on, girl,' he said. 'No sense in us freezing out here.'

Anna wholeheartedly agreed. She began to slosh her way along the muddy trail once more, stopping every minute to make sure Archie was still shuffling along behind her, trying to organise the wild thoughts spinning through her head. The Professor had taken them to a ghost town by the sea – where she had been attacked by the 'mayor' – and there had been something else hiding in the shadows, she was sure of it – something big, and hairy – and a lighthouse, too – *and a man beside the lighthouse, dressed all in grey.*

Anna froze mid-step, gripping the torch tightly. Archie was wearing a blue jumper, not a grey one – and hadn't he said he was the only resident for miles around? So who, then, had been watching her from under the tree?

Anna sighed. All she had wanted was a beach holiday – but already she could feel new mysteries tugging at her from the shadows, waiting to be un-picked. Even the weather was conspiring against her.

Whether she liked it or not, it seemed a new adventure had already begun.

—✝—

Anna had seen many strange things in her life, but never before had she walked through the ruins of a ghost town. The houses were like skeletons, stripped back to their wooden bones, desperately clutching at the roofs and fences that had not yet fallen to the ocean wind. Archie's torch shone easily through the rotting walls, blaring past worm-holes and fallen bricks, picking out the spooky details within: an empty cradle in one house; a grimy porcelain bathtub in the next. All of the gardens were completely overgrown.

They found the Professor and Max huddled together beside the one house that still seemed intact, shielding themselves from a fresh gust of rain. Max smiled at Anna as she approached, which she made a point of ignoring. She enjoyed watching him jump as Archie loomed out of the darkness, his long white hair blowing wild.

'Oh – there you are, Anna,' said the Professor, with only the faintest note of concern. 'I was just starting to worry.' He peered at Archie. 'I take it you must be Mr Silcock?'

'Archie's fine,' said Archie gruffly. He stuck his hand deep into his pocket, pulling out a large, rusty key. 'Glad you found the place all right. Open her up and I'll give you the tour.'

It was hard to believe that anyone would have bothered locking such a lonely house, but the Professor took the key and dutifully rattled it in the lock. With a nudge and a push, the door juddered open. Anna and Max rushed inside, both eager to escape the storm.

Immediately, something soft and sticky grabbed Anna around her face. She yelled in fright, spinning around as she slapped at her cheeks; Max shouted something unintelligible beside her, swatting at the air like a maniac. The Professor was gasping too, twirling on the threshold with his hands on his head, frantically clawing at his ears and nose.

'Ach, settle down, the lot of you,' said Archie. He pushed past them all, forcing his way into the centre of the room. 'You might as well have a look at what we're dealing with.'

He reached a hand to the low ceiling, deftly pressing a switch. At once the room was bathed in light – and then everyone but Archie began to scream.

The room was full of cobwebs. They hung from the roof like sails, stretching through the air in awful, spiky shapes, some as delicate as fine lace doilies, others as tangled as kite strings. An entire curtain of web had wrapped itself around Anna's head, sticking to her clothes, her skin, her hair; with a shudder of revulsion she pulled it from her face, flicking it away. Max and the Professor were still swiping at their own invisible snares. With all their twisting and turning, they looked rather like a pair of deranged ballet dancers.

'No need to be alarmed,' said Archie calmly. 'We'll soon get the place cleaned up. Find me a broom, and I'll knock away the worst of it.'

His entire body was wrapped thickly in webs, the sight of which made Anna feel faintly ill. She surveyed the room, looking past the cobwebs to the furniture beneath. On one side of the room sat a long wooden table surrounded by chairs, its surface buried under a precarious pile of cardboard boxes. On the other side stood two bookcases, their shelves crowded with papers, tools and knick-knacks. At the end of the room sat a large brick fireplace, dusty and cold, with a door on either side. Both of the doors were closed.

There was a feather duster on the nearest bookshelf. Anna dropped her bag on the ground and made a grab for the handle, wincing as a dirty grey cobweb wrapped around her arm. With a boldness she hoped she wouldn't regret, she swung the duster around her like a broadsword, messily collecting all the webs in her orbit. The room still looked filthy, but it did seem slightly less horrific than before.

'Oh, well done, Anna,' said the Professor, who had finally managed to clean himself off. 'That's much better.'

Anna threw the soiled duster into the corner. Her fingers were trembling. 'I thought you said we were going on a beach holiday,' she said. 'Not spending the night in a murder house.'

'Ach,' said Archie. 'I see you've told the children, then.'

The Professor's face went white. Max looked at him in concern, but his own face had paled as well, his brain still digesting what had been said. Anna turned slowly towards Archie, his last words hanging in the air more chillingly than any cobweb.

'What did you just say?' she whispered.

'I said, he's told you, then,' said Archie. 'About the deaths. About the curse. About poor old Madeleine Graves.' He paused, his white eyes glistening like diamonds. 'Surprised you came here at all, given the stories. There ain't nothing but ruin for those who spend a night in Mermaid's Purse.'

3

LOOSE LIPS

'I DIDN'T WANT TO ALARM YOU,' SAID THE Professor. 'And really, there's nothing to be alarmed about. As far as we know, nobody's even set foot in this place for over a year.'

Battle lines had been drawn across the living room. Anna and Max stood beside the bookshelves, united in anger, staring daggers at the Professor and Archie. The Professor was wringing his hands together, tapping his foot nervously against the wooden table. Archie Silcock looked unconcerned.

'You brought us to a *cursed* town,' said Max. 'A *ghost* town. We can't stay here. No way. Never in a million years.' He stamped his foot.

'I'm sure Mr Silcock was only joking about the curse,' said the Professor. 'There's no reason we can't stay here for a day or two.'

'Except for the spiders,' said Anna.

'And the dirt,' said Max.

'And the rats,' said Anna. 'Probably.'

Archie coughed. 'No reason to fear spiders,' he said. 'It's only the red-backs and the funnel-webs that'll do you any real harm, and they'll keep to themselves for the most part. You'll be fine.'

Anna stared at him in disbelief.

'Whose stuff is this, anyway?' said Max, gesturing to the cardboard boxes. 'This house isn't empty at all. Someone's been living here.'

'Well — yes,' said the Professor. 'I did rather hope that would be the case. I believe all these notes may have belonged to a famous academic. One of my heroes, in fact.' He smiled, unable to disguise his excitement. 'Madeleine Graves was a celebrated researcher long before I started digging around in musty libraries. Nobody knows what she was looking for when she flew to Australia — but if these notes belonged to her, then I might have the chance to continue her work.'

He ran a hand over the nearest box, his fingers twitching with anticipation. Anna felt her heart soften, just a little bit. If reading some old notes would make the Professor happy, then maybe — just maybe — spending a night in a ghost town wouldn't be such a terrible thing. They could chase away the spiders. They could clean up the dust.

It certainly wouldn't be the worst thing they'd ever done.

'What happened to Madeleine Graves, then?' demanded Max. 'Where did she go?'

The eagerness slipped from the Professor's face. He looked down at his feet, wringing his hands again.

'She vanished,' said Archie gruffly. 'Up and left this place, and never came back. Shame. She was a nice woman. Brought her some firewood in my handcart a few years back, when she first moved in. Stayed and had a drink with her. She could spin a good yarn.'

'And I'm afraid that nobody has seen Madeleine since,' said the Professor. 'At first she maintained an occasional correspondence with the university, but after a time she stopped contacting them altogether. Now they've sent me to try to recover her research.' His fingers twitched. 'Madeleine always had a talent for uncovering stories in the strangest of places. I do hope she didn't put herself in harm's way.'

Uncovering stories in the strangest of places. It seemed the Professor was already doing a fine job of emulating his hero. With a long sigh, Anna crossed the room and sat down at the table, pushing aside an overstuffed box. The table creaked.

'So, Madeleine came to – to Mermaid's Purse,' she said. 'That's the name of this town, right? And Archie, you think it's cursed. Why is that?'

'Ach,' said Archie. 'No sense in scaring you. *She* asked me the same question, when she was here. I'm sure the notes she took are lying round here somewhere.' He tapped his walking stick on the floor. 'Me, I'd best be getting home before the rest of the storm comes in. Should be safe enough from the worst of it in here. If it's dry enough for the spiders ...' He paused, reaching into his pocket. 'I've got some more torches here, and there should still be some firewood round the back. Get this place warmed up, and you'll be right as rain.'

He winked at no-one in particular. Anna wished she could ask him some more questions, but it seemed the old man had made up his mind to leave. She picked the worst of the cobwebs off his jumper as he shuffled to the door, following him onto the verandah as Max and the Professor called out their goodbyes.

'Bye, Archie,' she said. 'Thanks for bringing us the key.'

The old man nodded. Anna watched as he stared out at the darkened hills, taking in a deep breath of cold, salty air –

– and then suddenly his arm was lashing out, and his gnarled fingers were gripping her shoulder, pulling her towards him. Anna cried out, beating her fists against his chest, but then the old man's lips were at her ear, uttering urgent words.

'Take care, girl,' he whispered. 'Tread lightly. There's something wrong with this place –

something that doesn't agree with newcomers. Don't look for it. Don't speak of it. Stay away from it. And whatever you do, *keep the door locked tonight.*'

And then he was gone, hobbling away into the shadows, lost to the dark.

It took over an hour to purge the house of dust and grime. Max and the Professor brushed down the walls while Anna lit a fire in the cold brick hearth, Archie's words still whispering in her ears. No matter how hard she focused on the kindling, her gaze was constantly drawn back to the front door, her eyes lingering on the lock. She imagined a hundred different monsters bursting through the wooden panels, lunging into the room with their teeth bared, claws glinting, tails swiping through the air. But had Archie been talking about a monster, or had he only meant for her to beware of the so-called curse? What had he said to Madeleine Graves?

'That's marvellous, Anna,' said the Professor. 'We'll have the sausages cooked in no time.'

Anna blinked. A merry little fire was dancing before her, singeing her skin. She stumbled back from the hearth in a daze, shaking her head clear.

Max was kneeling in the corner beside one of the last cobwebs, a glass jar sitting on the floor beside him. An ant was pinched between the fingers of his ghastly right hand – the hand that had been killed not once, but twice, by wicked fairy magic. His fingers were clammy and pale, lifeless and blood-less ever since his encounter with the vampire in Transylvania, but there were also burn marks on his palm, ugly and black, still raw from his battle with the genie in Iran. Anna bit her lip as she stared at the dead hand, the beginnings of a bad feeling tickling at her stomach. Nobody at home had ever noticed Max's injury. Nobody knew what her brother had been through, fighting monsters and magic all across the world. Is that why he had tried to tell his friends about their adventures? Had he only wanted to share the burden?

Max threw the ant through the air. It fell into the centre of the cobweb and stuck there fast, wiggling its legs in terror as it tried to escape.

'Hey!' said Anna in alarm. 'What are you doing?'

Something was stirring in the shadows behind the bookshelf. Anna grimaced as a small black spider crept into the light, crawling cautiously towards the tangled-up bug. Then it sprang, darting across the old grey web, already spinning a new snare to finish binding its prey.

Max reached out with a dead finger and knocked the spider to the ground, quickly covering it with the glass jar. He slipped a piece of paper underneath the jar and flipped it back over, grinning in triumph at the spider trapped inside.

'Pretty cool, huh?' he said. 'I learnt how to do that at school.'

Anna scowled. 'No, it's not cool,' she said. 'It's cruel. You should let it go.'

'You're just jealous,' said Max. He tapped the side of the jar. 'You can use the knife on it if you want. Turn it into another pet for us to use.'

Anna glared at him. She shot a quick look at the Professor, who was busy unpacking sausages from a miniature esky, humming a happy tune. Max smiled smugly.

'Dad's not listening,' he said. 'And you can't talk to him about what's going on anyway. You heard what Archie said about this place. It *has* to be another fairy – a vampire, or a troll, or a genie, or even something we haven't seen before. And there's no-one else here, so if you want help solving this mystery, you have to talk to me.'

He tapped the jar again, watching as the spider scurried from one side to the other. Anna bunched her fists, trying to quench the fury that was building in her throat.

'Actually, I don't need any help,' she said. 'I've already started this adventure without you. Maybe you can join in on the next one.'

She smiled coolly at the stunned expression on Max's face. The bad feeling was tickling at her stomach again, but Anna forced herself not to care. She hadn't done anything wrong. Max was the one who'd tried to betray their secrets. Didn't he deserve to be punished?

'Fine,' said Max, his face turning red. 'Fine. Go on your stupid adventure. I don't care. I never wanted to keep that stupid knife anyway.' He held up the spider. 'I've got a new friend now. I might even let him go for a walk outside his house, after you're asleep. Hope he doesn't bite.'

He stomped across the room, the glass jar tucked ominously under his arm. Anna sighed, taking in a long breath, pushing the bad feeling out of her body. She didn't need Max. She didn't need anybody.

Strange things were happening in Mermaid's Purse, and Anna was determined to face them alone.

4

LOST PROPERTY

BEHIND THE TWO CLOSED DOORS WERE TWO ROOMS, each of them small and cobwebby. The room on the left contained a bed, a wardrobe and yet another bookshelf; the room on the right was filled entirely with junk. The Professor flipped a coin over dinner, which Anna called correctly; she smiled meanly at Max as he carried his bag into the junk room, dumping his things beside the thin foam mattress the Professor had set up. He did not look pleased.

There wasn't a bathroom. The Professor took them outside before bed to show them the old wooden outhouse, its rickety walls creaking in the wind. It didn't smell as bad as Anna had thought it might, but she still made up her mind to use the toilet as little as possible. The outhouse door did not have a lock.

The Professor, it seemed, would be sleeping in the living room, if indeed he slept at all. After dinner he had produced a large box of candles from his suitcase, lighting them around the table before switching off the overhead lamp. He placed another log on the fire as he bid the children goodnight, his eyes shining with the hunger of a bookworm in a library, ready to devour everything within.

Anna put a clean sheet and pillowcase onto the bed, coughing as a thick cloud of dust rose up from the bedsprings. She opened up the small, cramped window, blinking as a spray of rain blew into the room, savouring the freshness of the stormy breeze. Then she lay down on the bed, eyes closed, her fingers intertwined, thinking about everything that had happened so far. There was a man in grey — and a huge, dark, chittering thing — and now a woman as well, who'd vanished from the centre of a ghost town. And what about Archie's curse? Anna shivered as she thought about the word. Curses made her think of old, witchy objects, filled to the brim with dark and terrible magic. Now that she had entered the town, would she be cursed as well?

Maybe the answers were closer than she expected. Anna's eyes snapped open, a fresh new thought cutting through the rest. Madeleine Graves, a famous researcher, had already visited Mermaid's Purse. Whatever questions she was asking now, Madeleine had almost certainly asked them first.

The Professor was going to spend all night reading through the scholar's notes. Why couldn't she do the same?

The bookshelf beside her bed was smaller than the two in the main room, but it was still packed full of documents. Anna lit a candle and ran her finger along the first row of meticulously numbered files. A name caught her eye, printed neatly at the top of a thin yellow folder.

Archie Silcock.

Curiosity zipped through Anna's body. She pulled the folder from the shelf and opened it, quickly reading the handwritten note that was clipped inside.

Archie Silcock: 'The Mayor of Ghost Town'

Has lived in Mermaid's Purse all his life; only remaining resident. (Is this true?)

Suffered near complete vision loss aged 9: complication arising from insect bite.

Unfamiliar with local folk tales. (The huntress? The stone?)

Has documented local 'curse' for 60 years with the help of his sister, who lives further inland — see attached.

Has not heard of the Zeeduivel.

The rest of the folder was filled with newspaper clippings. Anna skimmed through the headlines, her breath catching in her throat as she read the same few words again and again. *Drowned. Diseased. Dead.* The clippings reminded her of another set of articles she'd read during her time in England, about the children who'd vanished beside a misty river. Those children, it turned out, had been eaten by a troll.

The pattern was horribly familiar.

Anna flipped back to the handwritten page, sounding out the unusual final word. She ran her finger along the files again, riffling all the way to the very end of the shelf. Wedged between the last folder and the shelf was a single note written on a tiny scrap of paper.

Zeeduivel – moved to wardrobe.

Anna frowned, turning slowly towards the closet. Why would a file be in there? She had so far made every effort to avoid disturbing the old cupboard for fear of what might be living inside – more bugs and spiders, probably, or even something larger, like a rat, or a bat, or a murderous kangaroo. But of course, that was a childish thing to think. There wouldn't really be anything dangerous inside. Anna went to the wardrobe and gripped the handle, wrenching open the door.

A saggy black arm flopped out from the darkness. Anna shrieked as the arm slapped at her neck; she dropped into a fighting stance, the white knife already in her hand, the magic blade filling her body with strength, with heat, with fire. She hefted the knife before her, ready to strike the arm — *the arm that didn't have a hand attached to it ...*

It was a wetsuit. Anna glared at the empty sleeve as she sheathed the knife, her nostrils smarting at the stale, salty smell wafting from the closet. The wetsuit was hanging beside a number of other web-draped outfits (most of them a rather striking shade of lime green), but at the bottom of the wardrobe was something very different: a large yellow oxygen tank, gathering dust in the corner beside a dirty wooden crate. Anna dragged the crate out into the candlelight, staring curiously at all the strange things gathered inside. On the top was a rubber diving mask, a crusty piece of seaweed still curled around the strap. Beneath the mask was a pair of flippers, and beneath the flippers were objects stranger still: old glass bottles in unusual shapes; a huge, rusted padlock; pieces of cutlery so black and dirty they might never be clean again. There was another file too, much fatter than the dossier on Archie Silcock. Anna removed it from the crate, glancing at the door. She knew she wasn't really doing anything wrong, but it still felt weird to be going through someone else's possessions. What if Madeleine Graves had written something she didn't want anyone else to read?

The first page in the new folder was a newspaper article in faded print. Anna sped through the text, holding the folder up beside the flickering candle.

A GRISLY DISCOVERY

SIGNS OF SHIPWRECK

Bones and debris have been washed ashore this week during cyclones near Mermaid's Purse. Boards, iron nails and portions of human skulls were found along the coast, which has recently been battered by a series of fearful storms. All items seem to have been long in the water.

Anna turned the page – and blinked in confusion.

The title of the next document seemed to have mixed itself up before her very eyes.

Vereenigde Oostindische Compagnie

Lijst Met Verloren Schepen

Anna groaned as she flipped through the rest of the folder, which was packed full of maps and charts. Nothing else was written in English: much like the Professor, it seemed Madeleine Graves had no trouble working in multiple languages. Anna selected a map at random and unfolded it onto the bed, puzzling over a craggy outline of Australia. After a minute of searching, she succeeded in finding the one word she was looking for. *Zeeduivel* was written beside a tiny cross, just off a particularly jagged piece of coast. The writing was so small and so cramped that it might have been mistaken for a smudge. Below the word was a number: *1622*.

'Why are you important?' whispered Anna. It felt good to break the silence in the room. 'Are you an island? Are you a code?' She flipped back to the newspaper article, scanning it again. 'No, of course you're not. You're a ship. A really, *really* old ship. Madeleine was investigating a shipwreck.'

But why? Anna frowned, trying to keep the facts straight. Was the shipwreck related to Archie's curse, or was it a dead end? Had she discovered anything important at all? Despite everything that had happened with Max, she suddenly found herself wishing she had someone to talk to.

No, you don't wish that at all, replied a mean voice at the back of her head. *You can do this on your own.*

Anna nodded to herself, stifling a yawn. There was just one more thing she wanted to check before she fell asleep – perhaps the most tantalising thing she'd heard since arriving in Australia. The town was called Mermaid's Purse, after all. Anna retrieved her rucksack from where she'd thrown it on the floor, ready to consult the book of fairy tales she'd packed right on top.

But the book was not there.

Anna stuck her arm deeper into the bag. The journal with the emerald green cover was still inside, as was the gnarled stone troll heart, and the small gold coin with the twisting face. But the old book of fairy tales had disappeared. With a rising sense of panic, Anna realised that her beautiful black scarf was missing, too: the black scarf that had been knitted just for her, to keep her warm on the coldest nights. Her bag of snacks was gone as well, and her good metallic water bottle was nowhere to be seen. Anna's heartbeat quickened as she upended the entire rucksack onto the bed, searching for her lost possessions.

And then she remembered her fall down the hill. She remembered how the torch had jumped from her hand – how the rucksack had bounced on her back as she fell – how quickly she had run through the mud and the slush. With dawning horror, Anna pictured the zipper on her bag jerking open, her beautiful scarf falling loose, her treasured book of fairy tales flying out into the night. Her possessions were lost outside, scattered along the long and winding path, soaking in the storm.

The weight of the loss crashed down on Anna's shoulders. The black scarf might have been okay out in the wet, but she knew for certain that the fragile book with the faded red cover would already be ruined. She fell onto the bed with a sob, tears sliding down her cheeks. How far had she walked with Archie? How far might the book have bounced off the path? What were her chances of finding it now?

It was no use. Anna threw herself under the covers as a sheet of lightning flared in the distance, sadness aching in her bones. Nothing else seemed to matter now: not curses, not shipwrecks, not anything. All that mattered was her lost book: the book she had carried with her for as long as she could remember.

Anna buried her head under her pillow, fighting back tears as the rain beat against the roof, weeping into the mattress as a piece of her childhood was washed away for good.

5

A TANGLED WEB

THE STORM RATTLED ON THROUGHOUT THE night. The rain came down in waves, falling soft, falling hard, never quite building into a true downpour. The candle on the bookshelf burnt low, the flame slowly drowning in an ocean of wax.

Anna stirred. She rolled across her tear-stained pillow, trying to stay comfortable, wishing herself back to sleep. After a minute, she rolled the other way. She tried to remember her dream: tried to remember where she'd been, who she was with. Then she rolled onto her back, lying very still, her legs pressed together tight. Nothing helped.

She needed to go to the toilet.

With a sleepy groan, Anna flung off the bed-covers, wincing as her feet touched the chilly floorboards. She noticed the clothes scattered around the room, and remembered with a start what had happened to her precious red book: but now the pain felt numb, like a bruise that was already a few days old. Anna cast the book from her mind, fumbling around in the darkness for Archie's torch, determined to make her trip to the bathroom as quick as possible.

The Professor was snoring quietly in the living room, his head resting comfortably on a thick sheaf of papers. Anna zipped her raincoat over her clothes as she tiptoed past. She unlocked the front door. She stepped outside.

At once a shower of rain splashed against her face, shocking her awake. Anna gasped, blinking around at the ghost town. Despite the rain, the night was surprisingly clear, the starlight picking out the world in neat shades of grey. Anna switched on Archie's torch anyway, shining it around the skeleton houses as she hurried to the outhouse. Strange shadows fell inside the neighbouring buildings, prickling her nerves, but whenever she looked more closely, there was never anyone there.

The toilet seat was icy cold. Anna held the door shut as she sat inside, flinching every time the wind blew through the rickety walls. For one terrifying moment, she thought she saw someone standing outside, watching her through the crack in the door; but when she stepped outside again the night was as lonely as before. Anna dashed back towards the house, glad her midnight adventure was over.

It was as she was passing the woodpile that she

saw the light. Anna stopped, and then kept going, hoping she hadn't seen anything; but then she stopped again and turned, staring out at the hills. Something was glowing faintly in the darkness, too bright to be a reflection, too low to be a star. It wasn't coming from the lighthouse, either. It was a few hundred metres away at most, on a hill near the sea. The light was pointing into town, shining feebly towards the house where Max and the Professor were still fast asleep. It was a light that made the hairs on Anna's neck stand up. It was a light that should not have been there at all.

Anna switched off Archie's torch and dropped it in her pocket, stepping behind the woodpile. Whoever was behind the light had surely seen her come out of the outhouse, but now she was hidden, safe in the shadows. Her mind churned through different possibilities, trying to guess where the light might have come from. Was it Archie again, back to deliver a forgotten warning? Was it Madeleine Graves, finally returning to her research? Or was it an escaped lunatic, come to break into the first house he could find? Anna shook her head, trying not to get spooked.

There was no reason for her to investigate the light. Sneaking around at night by herself was a bad idea – a bad, dumb, dangerous idea. She could get lost. She could get hurt. The smartest thing to do would be to run back inside and get into bed, and to search for clues in the morning.

But the heroes in her lost book wouldn't have gone to bed. Anna bit her lip, sneaking another look at the light. It wasn't that far away. It would be easy to creep a little bit closer. All she had to do was take the first step.

Anna zipped up her raincoat as high as it would go. She rubbed her hands together, thinking wistfully about her nice warm bed.

She made her decision.

The ground was soft under her feet as she stepped off the verandah. Rose thorns pulled at her shoes as she stole through the wild garden, slinking past fence posts and over a fallen clothesline, ducking in and out of a crumbling house with man-sized holes in its walls. She smiled to herself as she reached the side of the first hill, climbing silently up the slope as the wind pulled at her hood. Whoever had been watching her would have no idea where she was now. From the top of the hill she would be able to see them clearly: spy on them from behind, as they had tried to spy on her. Anna took each step carefully, digging her toes into the mud, determined not to slip back down.

The light was still shining when she reached the summit. Anna crouched down, her teeth chattering. The light was electric – she was sure of that – but she could see no-one else hiding out on the hills.

Anna dared herself to scramble even closer, sliding down one hill and scampering up the next. She could see the lighthouse again now, towering in the distance, a dark grey silhouette against a light grey sky. Had she strayed too far from town? But it was too late to turn back. The light was just ahead.

There was still nobody there. Anna stood up and walked over to the source of the light: a small electric torch. Anna frowned, her brain buzzing with confusion, trying to make sense of what she was seeing.

The light was coming from *her* torch – the very one she had thrown into the darkness, right before she ran into Archie. But she had met Archie on the other side of the lighthouse, much further from the sea. Could the storm really have blown the heavy torch this far? It didn't seem at all likely – and yet here it was, glowing in the night. Anna bent down and picked up the torch. The beam flickered on and off, just as it had done the last time she held it.

In the flickering light, Anna saw something else.

A new object was glinting from the darkness atop the hill. Anna froze, shining her old torch towards the *thing*, but the item was too small to see, hidden behind a tussock of grass. She went cautiously towards it, her feet sinking further into the earth. The hills were becoming sandier as she approached the ocean; she could already hear waves swelling behind the lighthouse, spraying salt into the air. She pulled her hood tight around her ears as she came upon the glinting object.

Sitting behind the tussock was her water bottle – the same one that had bounced out of her rucksack. Further along the dune was her lunchbox, still full of snacks, dry and uneaten. Anna slowly picked them up, feeling rather amazed. She was sure that this was not the way she had come into town, and yet here were her things, waiting patiently for her to find them. And there – there was her scarf! Anna stumbled up the next dune in delight, snatching the beautiful scarf into her arms. The fabric was sodden and cold, but still Anna hugged it to her chest, relieved that at least one great treasure had been returned to her.

She had walked for so long now that the towering lighthouse was not far away at all. Anna stared up at the building, taking in the large wooden door, the smooth stone walls, the unlit lantern. The tree beside the lighthouse rustled as the wind blew through its branches – and then something moved beside the trunk, causing Anna to jump in fright.

She was no longer alone.

The man in grey was standing beneath the lighthouse tree, rocking from side to side as the wind blustered around him. He was thin – impossibly thin – his arms long and spindly, his legs knocking together like reeds. His chest was stiff and rigid, but his pale head slowly swivelled towards Anna, freezing her in place with eyes she could not see.

It's a ghost, she thought, her heart hammering in her chest. *A ghost from ghost town.*

The grey man raised an arm, his ragged sleeve fluttering in the breeze. There was something clutched in his hand, too far away for Anna to see it clearly – something shaped like a rectangle. *A book.* Anna gasped, slapping the flickering torch, desperate to get a closer look. The grey man lowered his arm, nodding his head up and down.

Come to me, he seemed to say.

Could a ghost really have saved her book? Anna scurried towards the lighthouse as quickly as she dared. She could see the ocean now, endless and dark; the hiss of the tide crashed into her ears, whispering secrets she couldn't understand. The man in grey was standing with the moon at his back, waiting patiently for her, the old red book held out before him. Anna smiled with joy as she reached the lonely tree, her torch sputtering in her hand, reaching out to claim her prize.

A soft chittering sound rose up on the wind. Anna looked up as the tree branches shifted above her, bending and snapping, settling oddly against the trunk. The man in grey suddenly raised both his arms in the air – and then Anna was crying out, yelling as loudly as she possibly could, terror shooting through her veins.

There had never been a man in grey. An old skeleton was dangling limply under the tree, its body swathed in cobwebs, its torso thickened out with shells and driftwood. Each of its limbs was suspended on a piece of silver thread, swinging in the breeze, hanging from the branches like a rotting marionette. With a flood of disgust, Anna saw that her book of fairy tales had been lashed to its bony fingers.

The tree creaked loudly as the branches shifted their weight again. Anna took a step back as a long, hairy branch curled past her shoulder, hovering weirdly in the air. The old skeleton fell limp as other branches began to move as well, stretching out from their secret positions, extending wickedly into the night.

Except they weren't really branches. They were legs.

Anna screamed in horror as a giant spider stepped down from the tree, chittering with hungry delight, venom dripping from its fangs.

6

SECRETS AND LIES

THE SPIDER REARED BACK, ITS UNCURLED LEGS reaching higher than the treetop, its eight eyes glittering like mirrors. Fangs curved from its head like a pair of oily sabres, each one twisting inward to a deadly point. Its fat black abdomen swung low through the beach grass, as wide as a stone boulder, a silver thread trailing in its wake.

Anna managed to stagger backwards as the massive spider took a step towards her.

The spider reared back.

She knocked into the hoary skeleton, shuddering as the bones rattled in her ear like a demented wind chime. Without thinking, Anna dropped her old torch and snatched the book of fairy tales from the bony hand, sending the skeleton lurching through the air: and then she was running, sprinting towards the lighthouse as fast as she could, her lost possessions bouncing against her chest as she fled through the night. The box of snacks fell from her grasp as she stumbled over a branch; with one hand now free, Anna tried to unsheathe the white knife, grabbing awkwardly at the hilt. The chittering sound was close behind her, loud, angry, *excited*, but the lighthouse door was close as well, just a few steps away, so close she could almost –

The door was boarded up.

Anna moaned as a hairy brown leg brushed against her neck. She dashed around the side of the lighthouse, desperately trying to put something, *anything*, between her and the eight-legged night-mare. But on the other side of the lighthouse, there was only the sea. Anna threw the metal water bottle over her shoulder, hoping to distract the beast for one precious second. The white knife was still stuck in its sheath, tucked under her shirt, her jumper, her raincoat; Anna made another grab for the hilt as she tumbled down a split in the dunes, frantically wondering if spiders could swim, trying not to trip over as the sand grew wetter underfoot.

She had reached the beach. An angry tide rolled in to greet her, hissing as it slid across the sand, strands of black seaweed crawling in its wake. To the west stood a natural jetty of rocks, running all the way from the cliff into the cold, dark sea.

But the beach was not the safe haven Anna had been hoping for. The waves were tall and fast, smashing against the stone jetty with wild ferocity. Anna was a strong swimmer, but she could tell at once that swimming into the swell fully clothed would be a death sentence. So what was the better way to go? Would it be worse to drown, or to be eaten by a spider?

Anna stopped at the water's edge, her breathing ragged. She tucked the book of fairy tales into her waistband and wrapped the black scarf around her neck, shivering as the sodden fabric pressed against her skin. Then, with both her hands finally free, she unsheathed the white knife.

It had been a long time since Anna had drawn the knife out in the open. At home she looked at it often, laying it on her pillow and gazing in wonder at the pearly blade: but there was always something special about seeing the knife gleam under the stars, effortlessly catching the light on its edge. Anna held the knife aloft as she turned to face her foe, the blade shining like a silver teardrop. Was this the last time she would ever see it sparkle?

The spider was climbing silently down the dune, revelling in the thrill of the hunt. Anna squirmed as she stared into its ugly black eyes, feeling as if a hundred smaller spiders were wriggling under her skin. The beast was bigger than an elephant, its legs stretching out hideously around its enormous body. How many legs could she slice off before it caught her? Anna's arm began to tremble.

And then a voice called out to her from the darkness.

'*Hello!* Come here, quickly! You can hide with me!'

Anna gasped. The spider swivelled around, its foreleg twitching towards the row of craggy stones. Anna stared too, hardly daring to believe what she had heard. Had someone really come to save her?

'*Now!*' said the voice. 'In the rocks, by the water! *Be quick!*'

The spider charged. It scurried towards Anna in a fury of limbs, fangs clacking, venom spitting —

but Anna was already in flight. With all the energy she had left, she sprinted towards the stone jetty, the knife shining in her hand like a shooting star, yelping as a hairy leg pushed her in the back – *and now there was someone else on the beach*, waving at her with a thin, pale arm, reaching out from between two weather-beaten rocks. Anna screamed as another leg struck the sand beside her – gasped in pain as droplets of venom splattered against her neck – and then she was tumbling between the rocks, falling blindly into the space beyond, her head spinning from exhaustion.

'*Be still*,' whispered a voice from the shadows. 'She can sense your movement. Stay calm, and she might leave us.'

Anna swallowed hard, trying to control her breathing. The jetty rocks were stacked in a natural cave around her, with an entrance so narrow the spider could never hope to squeeze through. She lurched backwards as a single hairy leg extended through the gap, probing angrily at the air; with a small cry of surprise, she found herself splashing into a rock pool, falling hard against someone – against *something* – already inside. A pair of pale hands quickly wrapped around her body, covering her mouth, pinning her arms to her sides: Anna tried not to squirm as the spider's leg twitched in her direction, its claw extending through the darkness. How much could she trust the person in the water? She tried to relax as the pale hands dragged her further into the cave, away from the spider's leg, pulling her so deep into the rock pool that the water was lapping at her thighs.

The leg continued to hover. After a long moment, it dipped suddenly through the cave, striking the surface of the pool with the end of its claw. Icy water splashed into the air. The leg recoiled at once, disappearing through the stone door as quickly as it had come. Anna counted the seconds in her head, waiting for the leg to reappear, or for an awful fang to slide through the gap instead: but after one long, cold minute had passed, the spider had not returned.

The pale fingers dropped from Anna's lips. Anna gasped in relief, swiftly wading out of the chilly water, shivering all the way to her bones. She steadied herself against the damp stone wall, blinking in the darkness, turning to face her rescuer for the first time.

Sitting in the rock pool was a girl. She was a small, frail thing, her arms thin, her fingers delicate and white; but her long hair was a deep, dark black, the ends floating in the water like a tangle of kelp. For a second, Anna thought the girl might not be wearing any clothing; but then she blinked, and saw that the girl was wearing a bright green swimsuit, just like a set of bathers she had once owned. But why would anyone be swimming in the ocean so late at night? Anna frowned, trying to work it all out. Of course she was grateful to the girl for saving her – but what was she doing here?

'I think it's gone,' said the girl. 'We should be safe now.' She looked at Anna curiously. 'What do you think it was?'

Anna frowned. Wasn't it obvious they had just been attacked by a giant spider? She supposed the girl must not have seen everything that had happened on the beach. But then – her mind began to whir – *but then*, if the spider was yet another fairy monster, Anna *couldn't* tell the girl exactly what had happened, or else the fairies' attention might be drawn to the girl, putting her in danger too. She hid the white knife behind her back, trying to think of something to say.

'I – I don't really know,' she stammered. 'I didn't get a very good look at it. It was big, though. Really big. It chased me all the way from the lighthouse.'

The girl in the pool tilted her head. Her face was hidden in the shadows, but her eyes were bright, staring at Anna with great interest. She didn't look very scared. Then Anna blinked, and all of a sudden the girl *did* look scared, her eyes wide, her cheeks streaked with tears. Why hadn't she noticed that before? The fear she had felt as she fled from the spider was subsiding, but a new sense of unease was gnawing at the back of her brain. The girl in the pool was watching her closely.

'Well, that's odd,' said the girl slowly. 'That thing was very close behind you. I thought you would have had a good look at it.' She paused. 'Unless you're keeping it a secret? That would be interesting. I like secrets.' Her eyes gleamed as she stared out from the darkness. 'What's that in your hand?'

Anna winced, wishing she'd hidden the knife sooner. She tried to hold it even further behind her, hoping that the blade had lost some of its shine.

'It's nothing,' she said. 'Just a bit of metal I picked up. To protect myself.'

The girl raised her eyebrows. She ran a hand through the water, leaving a trail of ripples in its wake. It looked as if she was thinking. Anna decided she'd better take control of the conversation.

'I'm staying here with my family,' she said. 'In Mermaid's Purse, just over the hill. I got a bit lost tonight, that's all. But it's funny, because Mermaid's Purse is supposed to be a ghost town. Nobody lives here. And yet ...'

She let the sentence peter out, hoping it hadn't sounded too much like an accusation. The girl in the pool remained perfectly still, the tendrils of her black hair floating back and forth. Then she smiled, her white teeth glinting in the moonlight.

'That *is* funny,' she said. 'Because *my* family have been living here as well, and we didn't think any-one lived here either. And yet here we are together, meeting each other in the middle of the night. It's so *unusual*.' Her eyes shone a little brighter. 'It's a secret, just for us. This town has so many secrets. It's an utterly delicious place.'

There was something strange about the girl's smile. Perhaps her teeth were too sharp, or her lips were too thin. Or maybe the problem was that she sometimes didn't look very much like a girl, but rather like some scaly, salty thing that had floated up from the ocean floor. And yet she *was* a girl. In a way, she looked like all of Anna's friends at once, their features combined into one perfect human face.

So why was she still sitting in the freezing rock pool?

'You look tired,' said the girl kindly. 'You should go and rest. We can meet each other again tomorrow, if you like.' She splashed the water with delight. 'We can tell each other more secrets. Do you know what's there in the bay, hidden by the reef? If you come back, maybe I'll show it to you.'

Anna nodded slowly, looking down at her book of fairy tales. She did want to meet the girl again – wanted to ask her all sorts of questions when her body wasn't aching, when her brain wasn't so sluggish. Something about the girl didn't seem right: their conversation so far had felt like walking a tightrope, with secrets and lies balanced carefully on either side. In the warm light of day, maybe she could get some answers.

But first she had to make it home. Anna peered outside as a heavy wave of rain began to fall, leaking through the stone roof in drips and dribbles. It was the start of a gale, the first wet taste of the downpour to come. The tide rushed in with a delighted roar, the swell already fat with raindrops. There was no sign of the spider.

'Oh, that's helpful,' said the girl. 'Whatever was chasing you probably won't come out in the rain.

You'll be able to walk home safely.'

'Mmm,' said Anna. She squeezed the white knife. 'You might be right.'

The girl smiled. 'It's settled, then. We'll meet back here tomorrow morning, and I'll tell you everything I know about this place. All the secrets. All the hidden things. It'll be tremendous fun.' Her smile widened. 'My name is Sylvie. What's yours?'

Anna stepped outside the cave. The rain fell hard against her face, waking her up, washing away her confusion. She looked back at the girl sitting in the rock pool: the girl who was not wearing a green swimsuit; the girl who had never been crying; the girl who was almost certainly not a girl at all.

Do not tell a fairy your real name.

'Rose,' she said. 'My name is Rose.'

And then she was gone, racing along the beach, her long black scarf whipping in the wind behind her.

7

MESSAGE IN A BOTTLE

'MY WORD, THESE SAUSAGES ARE DELICIOUS,' said the Professor. He looked at the children with bleary eyes, his hair a mess. 'Did you sleep well?'

He tucked back into his meal without waiting for an answer. Max mumbled something in agreement, munching on his own sausage, tomato sauce smeared across his lips. The spider in the jar sat on the floor beside him, the spider tapping on the glass with a spindly black leg. Anna tried not to look at it.

She had not slept well. Her journey back to town had been completely nerve-racking: a terrifying series of stops and starts, frights and false alarms, desperate dashes from one hiding spot to the next. In the end, none of it had mattered. She hadn't seen a trace of the beastly spider. Even the foul skeleton-puppet had disappeared, no doubt dragged away to some secret lair. Maybe the girl in the cave had been right. The spider did not seem to like the rain.

The good news, then, was that the rain was still falling heavily. Every so often a stormy draught would whistle through the walls, catching a stack of papers and blowing them through the air; the Professor had quickly become adept at finding unusual paperweights, including the greasy frying pan he had used to cook breakfast. But there was nothing he could do about the creaking of the floorboards, or the rattling of the doorframes, or the leaks that had sprung up beside the fireplace. The wind was so fierce that it sometimes felt as if the little house was about to be blown away.

'We can play something today, if you want,' said Max timidly. 'I found an old board game in my room. I think some of the pieces might be missing, but it could still be fun. If you felt like it.'

Anna ignored him. She flipped through her book of fairy tales as she ate her breakfast, cracking open the pages that had been stuck together with damp. She had read the book many times before, poring over the descriptions of monsters magical and macabre, and so she already knew that the book would tell her nothing about spiders, or shipwrecks, or skeletons hanging on strings. But Anna was looking for something else. She stopped chewing as she found the right page, frowning in concentration.

Like the crossroads found in forests, plains, and caves, the deepest oceans have been known to contain intersections between the worlds. The fairies of the water bleed easily between these realities, their features spliced evenly between the humanoid and the marine. These fairies covet secrets above all else and have a fondness for sunken treasures, hidden as they are in the depths of the sea. They have been named variously as merrow, rusalki, *and* maneli, *but tend to be best known as* ...

CRASH!

The frying pan had fallen off the table. A sheaf of papers flew into the air, carried up by the draught, fluttering out across the room. The Professor jumped up in alarm as a page of notes glided towards the open fire, skewering a paper with his plastic fork.

'Oh dear,' he said. 'Help me gather these up, will you? Quickly now!'

Anna snapped her book shut, hurrying to pick up the nearest papers. Some of the notes were written in the Professor's familiar scrawl, but she also recognised the neat handwriting of Madeleine Graves from the folders in her bedroom. Were there clues hidden in these notes as well? Anna scanned each page as she picked it up, but there were no mentions of the *Zeeduivel*. Maybe the Professor didn't even know about the shipwreck at all.

'What's this one about?' said Max. He was holding up an old piece of parchment, yellow at the edges, a spindly shape drawn across its centre. 'The picture looks cool.'

The Professor made a funny squawking sound. He crossed the room in an instant, carefully prising the parchment from Max's fingers and laying it back on the table. He pinned the corners down with a handful of pencils, gently smoothing out the creases, his tired eyes shining with excitement.

'*This* is something special,' he said. 'According to her notes, Madeleine found it in a curiosity shop on the other side of the world, rolled up inside an old glass bottle. It's by far the oldest document in her collection here – maybe four hundred years old, or thereabouts. It must be worth a fortune!'

Anna walked over to the table, her curiosity piqued. Max leant over the parchment, doing his best to block her view, but the Professor beckoned her forward, forcing Max to step aside.

'What's your problem?' Max said as Anna's face turned white. 'It's not that scary.'

On the parchment was a picture of a spider. The drawing looked rushed, as if the artist had been working at great speed, but there was no mistaking the long hairs that speckled the spider's legs, or the wicked curve of the creature's jet black fangs. Anna stared in astonishment at the horrible picture, her mouth open wide. Had someone else really managed to see the spider?

'It's rather remarkable, isn't it?' said the

Professor, mistaking her silence for awe. 'I've never seen a drawing of an antipodean animal as old as this. But it's the writing that's got me truly baffled. Having them both here together – why, it's unlike any artefact I've ever seen!'

Anna peered closer. Lines of text had been printed between the spider's legs and around its body, squashed into whatever space remained on the paper. It looked as if the words had been written rather quickly too, but each letter was still neat and elegantly formed, like the writing people had done with quills in the olden days. Anna squinted at the first line, trying to read it aloud.

'*De jager kwam uit de grond,*' she began. '*En ze zal terugkeren naar de grond. Ze zal haar steen vinden, en ze zal groeien, en ze zal slapen* ... what does that mean, then?'

'It's a story,' said the Professor. 'An old fairy tale, about a monstrous spider. Quite fanciful, of course, but it's exactly the sort of thing Madeleine was interested in. Isn't it grand?'

He looked slightly taken aback by the appalled expression on Anna's face. Anna was speechless. She knew Madeleine Graves had been searching for a shipwreck – but had the scholar really known about the giant spider as well? She waved her hands for the Professor to continue; he promptly sat down at the table, looking rather flustered.

'Er, well, yes – I haven't quite finished my translation,' he said. 'But I believe the story starts with the spider coming here from another world. It crawled here through the earth, you see, and there was so little food underground that it had grown thin and hungry – all the better to squeeze itself through caves and caverns. But it was still big – very big – when it reached the surface. It was bigger than any other animal: bigger than the trees, almost as big as the hills.'

Max scoffed. 'That's a bit preposterous.'

But Anna couldn't stop listening. Time and time again, old fairy tales had given her the information she needed to defeat monstrous fairies. This story wasn't in her book – but didn't it make sense for the spider to have emerged from the same twisted place as all the other monsters? She shushed Max, nodding at the Professor to keep talking.

'Well, once the spider reached the surface, it began to hunt,' said the Professor. He seemed to be warming to his audience. 'And it ate all the animals it could find on the land. Birds, lizards, marsupials – the whole lot. It ate and ate, and as it ate it grew, and soon its hunger became truly insatiable. The whole country was in danger, because if the spider could not be contained, then every last living thing would be consumed.'

'Creepy,' said Max. He picked up his glass jar, holding his tiny black spider beside Anna's ear. 'I wonder how many bugs I'll have to feed to this guy before he can eat you.'

'Shut up,' said Anna. She was feeling breathless now. Every gust of wind made her feel like the giant spider was just outside, rattling the shack with its massive legs so the Professor wouldn't spill its secrets. What was the monster's weakness? 'Please, keep going,' she said to the Professor.

But the Professor was staring intently at the edge of the parchment, trying to make out some words in blotted ink. His lips opened and closed, stumbling over the spoiled words.

'Professor?' said Anna urgently. 'What does it say?'

'Um – well, I'm not entirely sure,' said the Professor. 'This final section will require some restoration, I think. But it appears the spider became so hungry that it attempted to eat the world. It filled its empty belly with stone, and its body grew so heavy that it began to turn to stone itself. And then the spider slept, and its body was transformed into the ocean rocks, and the beaches, and the hills.' He frowned. 'But I'm not sure I'm telling this in the right tense – this might be the tale of an event yet to come. I'm afraid my Dutch is a little rusty.'

'*Dutch?*' said Max. He screwed up his face. 'Aren't we in Australia?'

'Yes, we are.' The excitement returned to the Professor's voice. 'And that really is the most remarkable thing of all. It seems this is an original Australian fairy tale, cooked up by some of the very first European explorers to set foot in this land. I think their ship must have landed right here, in Mermaid's Purse – and when they came ashore and saw the size of the local spiders, they invented this fabulous document. It's astonishing. It's amazing. I've never seen anything like it.'

He sat back and sighed, his eyes misting over.

Anna didn't think the Professor would have looked quite so relaxed if he knew how big the local spiders really were. She tried to picture the Dutch sailors stepping onto the beach, staring around in awe at the strange land down under. Would the sailors have met any of the local people when they landed? Anna imagined the two groups huddled together on the dunes as an eight-legged terror stalked them from the shadows, the locals trying to warn the sailors of the terrible danger, the Dutch desperately trying to return to the safety of their ship. She doubted many of the sailors had survived. She shivered as she imagined them being picked off one by one over a long, cold night, until the warm light of day had finally delivered them salvation.

But the Dutch hadn't escaped. Anna shut her eyes, concentrating hard as three separate stories converged in her mind. According to the map in her bedroom closet, a ship had sunk off the coast of Mermaid's Purse, lost for almost four hundred years. That, surely, was the ship of explorers the Professor was imagining: the explorers who had learnt of the giant spider, and lived just long enough to write their story on a piece of parchment. But where had the story come from? Anna knew for a fact the ending wasn't true. The spider wasn't made of stone – it was alive, cursing the land with its very presence. And yet, when Madeleine Graves had found the sailors' story, she had thought it was so important that she had travelled all the way to a dismal death trap by the sea. So why had she wanted to find the sailors' shipwreck? That seemed to be the last big secret left.

Luckily for her, Anna had already scheduled an appointment with the girl who claimed to know all the secrets in town.

Max cried out in annoyance as Anna pushed past him. She picked up her breakfast plate and strode over to her bedroom, lost in thought.

'Hey!' said the Professor. 'Where are you going?'

Anna turned around. 'I think I'll go for a walk,' she said. 'Not far,' she added, as the Professor opened his mouth. 'Just up the hill, so I can have a look at the beach in the daylight. I'll wear a jumper and a raincoat, and I won't go anywhere near the water. I'll be back before you know it.'

She ran into her room before the Professor could say another word. She knew he wouldn't really mind if she went outside; he never really minded what she did, so long as he had an old book to bury his nose in. Besides, she didn't have time to argue. There was a lot of work to do.

Firstly, she had to send for help.

Anna went to her bedroom window and lifted it open, rolling her eyes as a gust of rain sputtered inside. She set her paper plate on the windowsill, weighing it down with a bookend from the bedside shelf. On top of the plate sat her half-eaten sausage, its skin delicious and crisp.

Anna closed her eyes, and thought about the cat.

The cat. Anna and Max had seen many mysterious things over the past six months, but their encounters with the small black cat remained one of the most mysterious things of all. They had first met the cat in England, where it had spied on them as they followed the fearsome trail of the troll; and then it had appeared again in Iran, leading them safely through the desert in their darkest hour. Anna had called for the cat many times since, leaving a saucer of milk beside the back step every night, but although she had attracted many stray animals to their door, she had never again seen the mysterious feline with the golden eyes and electric blue whiskers.

But maybe the cat had seen her. Maybe it was still

out there, watching from the edges of the world, waiting until she was in peril once more. Didn't it seem like the perfect time for the cat to appear again?

'Hi,' said Anna. She spoke into the rain, letting the wind carry her voice away. 'Hello. It's me, Anna.' She opened her eyes, feeling rather self-conscious. 'I've brought you a sausage. And last night, I got chased by a giant spider.'

A sudden gust whooshed through the window, almost knocking the sausage off the plate. Anna tucked it under the bookend as well, trying to make the whole thing look as appetising as possible.

'You don't have to help me,' she continued. 'But I'd like it if you did. You seem like a friend – a friend I can trust. I'd love to see you more. Learn more about you. If you felt like it.'

There was no response. Anna crossed her arms, trying to stay warm. Was the message working, or was she talking to herself?

'Okay,' she said. 'That's all. I'm going to go and talk to a girl I met last night. I think she might be a mermaid. Could be dangerous. Come along, if you're interested.'

And with that, she packed her bag, put on her raincoat, and walked out the door.

8

THE DEEP BLUE SEA

THE AIR OUTSIDE WAS WARMER THAN ANNA HAD expected. The sun was peeking out from behind the clouds, lighting the hills with a gentle glow. Rain speckled her coat as she climbed the path she had taken the night before, keeping a watchful eye on her surroundings. Fortunately, there did not seem to be anywhere for the spider to hide. The hills were bare.

But danger was still lurking somewhere nearby – Anna was sure of it. She glanced over her shoulder as she circled the lighthouse, the grass rustling in her ears. Had it been a mistake to leave the house a second time? It would have been so easy to stay indoors: to make up with Max and play his stupid board game, or to read old stories with the Professor until the sun went down. There was no need for her to talk to the girl from the pool again. Nobody in her family had been kidnapped, and the world didn't seem to be in any great peril. So why was she so determined to keep risking her own safety?

Because that's what Madeleine Graves would do. The answer floated up from the back of Anna's mind. She had never met the lost scholar – had never even seen a picture of her – but she couldn't help but feel as if she and Madeleine were both driven by the same indomitable curiosity. Something weird was unfolding by the seaside, in the ghost town filled with secrets and lost things. To ignore the call to adventure would be unforgivably boring. The mystery needed to be solved.

Anna smiled to herself as she stepped onto the beach, the wet sand squelching beneath her shoes. She made a beeline for the stone jetty, ducking through the gap into the gloomy cave. There was nobody there. Anna frowned and walked back across the beach, idly following a trail of bird tracks towards the shallows.

'You came back!' cried a voice from the water. 'Splendid. I knew you would.'

Anna squinted out at the ocean. The girl named Sylvie was swimming in the break, her dark hair coiling through the water like an ink spill. She waved a pale hand as she swam towards the shore.

'You can come in, if you like,' she called. 'The water's lovely.'

Anna very much doubted that it was. She stood resolutely on the beach as Sylvie drifted closer, staring intently at her face, her hands, her hair.

Once again, the girl did not appear to be wearing any clothing – and then it looked as if she was wearing a green swimsuit – and then, when Anna *really* narrowed her eyes, it suddenly looked as if the girl was wearing nothing but a string of glistening necklaces, made from rows and rows of shiny white needles. There were bracelets decorating her wrists as well, each one made of the same strange material. Anna could not remember ever having seen such peculiar jewellery.

The girl's skin was unusual, too. In the darkness of the cave, Anna had thought she was pale, but in the dim morning light, her skin looked positively translucent. As Sylvie approached the beach, Anna felt as if she could almost see right through her, peering between her ribs to see the waves crashing behind. It was an odd thing to see (or to almost see), and it made Anna feel rather uncomfortable. She did her best to focus on the girl's face instead, hoping Sylvie's cheeks would remain opaque.

'I'm glad you made it here safely,' said Sylvie. She had stopped in the shallows, her legs hidden by the water, smiling coyly through her tangled hair. 'The thing that chased you must be sleeping in today. That's good.'

Anna nodded. She looked closely at the waves, trying to spot the girl's feet, but the clouds were casting a dark shadow on the sea. Could she ask the girl to show them to her? Anna summoned up her nerve.

'I'm here to swap secrets,' she said boldly. 'You told me there was something hidden in the bay. I'd like to know what you meant.'

Thunder rumbled on the horizon. Anna jumped without meaning to, looking around in concern. For a second she thought she saw something moving atop the dune, but when she squinted it was gone, lost in the swirling rain. When she looked back around, Sylvie was smiling widely, showing off her sharp white teeth.

'Oh, yes,' she said. 'The hidden thing. I know all about that. I could show you where it is. I could even take you all the way in.' She pouted. 'But you said you wanted to swap secrets. What secrets do you have for me?'

Anna grimaced. This was it. It was time to throw caution to the wind.

'Well,' she said, 'I know quite a few secrets, actually. You see, I know all about the fairies. I've met a vampire, and a troll, and quite a few genies. I even know where you come from. The old wood.'

She tried to say the words with confidence, but the last part was a gamble. Despite their many monstrous adventures, she and Max had never learnt much about the fairy world – only its name, muttered again and again in each country they visited. Even Caspar, their genie friend from Iran, had refused to tell them any more about it, answering their questions (and, later, their letters) with a dignified silence. For all the secrets they had learnt since their trials in Transylvania, it seemed that some magical knowledge would always be forbidden.

But Sylvie didn't know any of that. Anna felt a rush of excitement as the girl's eyes widened, unable to believe the secrets Anna was spilling. She decided to seal the deal.

'And, of course, there's this.' With an elegant flourish, Anna drew the white knife from its sheath, pointing the blade up towards the storm. As if in reply, a crack of lightning forked across the heavens; at once the knife began to gleam with an electric shimmer, sending a buzz of adrenaline through Anna's bones. She grinned meanly, revelling in the power, enjoying the shocked expression on Sylvie's face. She knew that the other girl hadn't expected her to have a secret like this.

Sylvie composed herself quickly. She dipped under the water, tossing her head back and forth. When she emerged, her great mass of hair was gathered behind her, leaving her face clear and bright. She fixed Anna with a malevolent stare, her eyes a fearsome blue. Anna felt her confidence fading away.

'So,' said Sylvie. 'You *did* see the spider. I wasn't sure, you know. I thought you might be in denial.' Her lips curled into a smirk. 'She's always been good to us. Keeps the hills nice and empty, so no-one sees us swimming about. There's only one of you she likes, and he's as blind as stone. I think she keeps him as a pet.'

Sylvie stared at Anna calmly, as if this news was the most normal thing in the world. Anna managed to smile back, hoping she didn't look as sick as she felt, her brain still processing all the horrible things the girl had just said. She imagined Archie Silcock wandering blindly over the hills, unaware of the great spider walking right beside him. The file in her bedroom had said Archie had lost his vision because of an insect bite. Could it be that the spider had chosen Archie as a pet when he was only nine years old – the same age Max was now?

'I'm surprised you made it back here a second time,' continued Sylvie. She seemed to be enjoying Anna's discomfort. 'These hills are riddled with her tunnels. Some of her trapdoors are so well-hidden that not even I can see them. But it's true that she doesn't like the water. If you'd come here on a clear day, I bet she'd have snared you like a ...'

She trailed off, her head flicking back to look at something past Anna's shoulder. Anna spun around, fearing the touch of a fang on her neck, but the beach seemed to be just as deserted as before. Sylvie, however, was now scowling in earnest. She pointed a pale finger at the nearest sand dune, her blue eyes wild.

'A spy!' she cried. 'Someone is perched there, listening to our secrets! You must capture them, quick!'

Anna looked around again, raising her hand to keep the rain off her face. It was hard to spot anything against the rippling grey sky. The only thing she could see on the dunes was more spinifex: grassy tussocks thrashing this way and that, tufts sweeping back and forth ...

And then, to her horror, she saw another tuft – a tuft of brown hair, poking out above the grass. The owner of the hair tried to duck out of sight, but Anna had already recognised him. She wrinkled her nose in indignation.

'You!' she yelled.

There was a small yelp from atop the hill. Anna glared as the little face popped up again, clearly still hoping he might not have been seen. Then, with a groan of resignation, the spy stood up, slowly making his way down the sandy path. His cheeks were flushing red as he crossed the beach.

'Who is that?' hissed Sylvie. She sank low in the water, hiding her body from view. 'You must get rid of him!'

Anna sighed. 'I wish I could,' she said. 'But I think I'm stuck with him for life.' She scowled. 'He's my brother.'

Sylvie's eyes seemed to widen further still, but she kept silent as Max shuffled towards them. Anna gave Max her most withering look, trying to think of a mean remark. To her disappointment, it was Max who managed to speak first.

'Dad said I could follow you,' he said. 'He said to make sure you didn't get into any trouble. I didn't *want* to follow you, if that's what you're thinking.' He cast a nervous glance at Sylvie. 'And I *definitely* didn't know you were meeting someone.'

He looked down at his feet, blushing furiously.

Anna gritted her teeth, cursing Max's timing. She needed Sylvie to keep talking – needed her to keep divulging all the secret things she knew. Didn't Max realise he was about to scare the girl away?

Luckily for her, Sylvie no longer appeared to be upset. She bobbed her head out of the shallows, a curious smile playing on her lips, examining Max from head to toe. Her gaze came to rest on his grisly right hand.

'Oh my,' she said. 'You're *dead*. I've never seen anything so horrible.'

Max flinched. He stepped closer to Anna, stuffing his hands deep into his pockets. Sylvie smirked at him as a spark of realisation flickered across his face.

'Oh,' he said. 'You're a – you're a *thing*. A fairy.'

Anna could hear the fear in his voice. She thought about touching his arm to let him know everything was okay, but she was worried Sylvie might think the gesture was some sort of signal. She smiled at Max instead, but he didn't see it.

'You're right,' said Sylvie. 'I am a thing. I'm the keeper of the secrets. But I don't have any secrets for a dead boy.' She pointed at Anna. '*We're* going for a little adventure, and there's only room for two. I'm afraid you'll have to stay behind.'

She bared her pointed teeth as Max's face stiffened. He turned to look at Anna, confusion burning in his eyes.

'What's going on?' he said. 'Who is she? Why didn't you tell me about her?' The fear in his voice was fading; he was starting to sound upset. 'You don't really want me to go, do you, Anna?'

His final word flew through the air like an arrow. Anna felt it shoot through her chest, cutting through her flesh, her bones, her blood. Suddenly she felt as if some vital element had been sliced from her body: as if her heart had been pitched out into the sea, freezing and cracking as it dropped beneath the icy waves. In a daze she turned around to find it, sure that she would see her heart lying on the ocean floor: but there was only Sylvie, her eyes blazing with fire, her hair flying up into the storm, her face split open with a terrifying grin.

Do not tell a fairy your real name.

Anna stood up very straight. She stared down at Max, a strange tingling on her lips.

'Go,' she said, in a voice that didn't quite seem like her own. 'We don't want you here, and we never will. Go home, and don't ever come back.'

The storm was loud, but her words seemed to ring out even louder. Max looked stunned. He opened his mouth, but no sound came out. Anna watched coldly as he turned slowly away, pulling his hood down to his nose, his shoulders sinking in defeat.

'Bye, then,' he said huskily. 'I guess I'll see you later.'

Anna didn't reply. She stood completely still as Max shuffled away across the sand, suddenly feeling rather confused herself. She knew she'd said something to upset Max, but she couldn't quite remember what it was. And shouldn't she have told him something else? Wasn't there a warning she should have given him?

'Perfect,' said Sylvie, interrupting her thoughts. 'We've got the whole beach to ourselves. Now I can show you the biggest secret of all.'

She clapped her hands, her eyes gleaming.

'Come into the water, Anna,' she said. 'It's time to go for a swim.'

9

BLOOD AND WATER

LATER, ANNA WASN'T ABLE TO RECALL THE moment she walked into the ocean. She didn't remember shrugging off her scarf and raincoat, or kicking off her shoes; nor did she remember her first tentative step into the swash, when the water must surely have chilled her toes to the bone. Her next memory was of a wave crashing over her face, choking her as the freezing water spilled into her nostrils. She realised with a start that a pale arm was holding her around the neck, gently pulling her across the sea. A tangle of black hair was dangling over her shoulders.

'Don't struggle,' said Sylvie in a soothing voice. 'We don't have far to go. Just relax.'

Anna didn't feel the slightest bit relaxed. She struggled as best she could, trying to slither out of Sylvie's grip, but the other girl held her tight, her arm locked like a vice. As she tilted her head, Anna spied the lighthouse in the distance, a tiny silhouette on the horizon. The sight made her panic even more. They had already gone too far – swum further from the shore than could possibly be safe. If lightning struck the ocean anywhere nearby, it would electrocute them for sure.

'We have to go back,' Anna gasped. 'We're in too deep!'

Sylvie laughed. 'This ocean is so deep, it could

swallow your entire world,' she said. 'But I'm not taking you to the bottom. The reef is up ahead – can you see it? We'll be there soon. You must calm yourself, *Anna*.'

And suddenly Anna did feel calm. She looked down at herself in polite bewilderment as all her muscles went numb, as if a doctor had just injected her with anaesthetic. It was a strange sensation, and not a pleasant one. Anna frowned as her arm flapped idly in the waves, her hand swimming along like a bizarre pink fish. Hadn't she just been worried about something? She tried to think, but the thoughts in her head felt foreign and weird. It reminded her of how she'd felt standing on the beach, when she'd spat out the words she couldn't remember – *the words she'd spat out just after Max had said her real name* ...

'We're here,' said Sylvie softly.

She released her hold on Anna's neck. Anna

spluttered as her head sank beneath the water. She kicked as hard as she could, popping back above the surface, wincing as the saltwater pricked at her eyes.

'Swim over that way,' said Sylvie. 'You should be able to stand up there.'

Anna scowled as a wave splashed over her face. How could she stand up in the middle of the ocean? She paddled half-heartedly in the direction Sylvie had suggested. To her surprise, her knee bumped up against something solid, hidden below the blue-black water. Anna eased her body onto the craggy shelf at once.

'Why did you bring me here?' she moaned. 'What's going on?'

A terrible anxious feeling was tightening around her chest. She could just make out the lighthouse in the distance, so far away now that she could never hope to swim there on her own. The current was already pulling at her legs, trying to pluck her from her perch; Anna dug her fingers into her peculiar seat, holding on for dear life.

'You *wanted* to come here,' said Sylvie. She looked at Anna innocently, her blue eyes bright. 'You told me you wanted to learn about the thing hidden in the bay. This is the reef where it sank. The shipwreck.'

The shipwreck. Anna stared dubiously at the gloomy water, trying to regain her composure. She didn't trust Sylvie – not one bit – but there was still a tiny chance that the girl might be trying to help her, in her own strange way. But what good was visiting the reef if she was stuck up at the surface?

'I can't see anything,' she said. 'The water's too dark. We'll have to go back.'

Sylvie smiled. 'Oh, no,' she said. 'I want to show it to you properly. It's beautiful, really, and you don't have to swim very deep to find it. Even you could make it down there with a bit of help. All I have to do is give you a little gift.'

She swam over to Anna's side, brushing up against her sodden pants. Anna tried to flinch away, but she really didn't have anywhere else to go. She didn't want a gift. A shiver ran up her spine as Sylvie gently took her hand, squeezing her fingers tight.

'Lean down to me,' whispered Sylvie. 'Lean down to me, *Anna*.'

Anna's ears twitched as the fairy girl said her name. She could feel her mind starting to change again; suddenly she *did* want to lean down, to put her face close to the water, to receive Sylvie's gift as quickly as possible. But that wasn't right. Something was wrong with her head – something big; something serious. Anna clenched her teeth, trying to hold onto her own thoughts.

'Too late,' said Sylvie.

Without warning, she pulled hard on Anna's

hand, throwing her completely off-balance. Anna shrieked as she fell into the sea, floundering as a wave crashed against her. Then Sylvie's face was pressed against her arm, the girl's sharp white teeth biting hard into her flesh, and Anna's cries were stifled as a cold rush of saltwater began to pour into her throat. She kicked out, lashed out, hoping to strike one of Sylvie's perfect blue eyes, but now her lungs were burning, drowning her from the inside out, dragging her down with their newfound weight. With a final burble, Anna's head dipped beneath the surface; she tried to burst back up, but Sylvie was holding her fast, pulling her down into waters dark and deep. Anna opened her mouth and screamed, flailing in terror as her very last air bubble flitted away.

And then she breathed in, and everything was black.

Anna had never thought much about dying. There had been moments on previous adventures when she had felt sure her life was about to end, cut short by the sharp bite of a vampire, or the crushing jaws of a troll; but those moments had passed quickly, her fear cast aside in the elation of victory. She had never really wondered what might have happened if the monsters had triumphed instead. Life was too much fun to worry about what might come next: about the places her mind might go when her body could no longer carry on. Death had always felt like something that only happened to other people.

Evidently, she had been wrong.

The experience was a lot more peaceful than she had expected. It was cold – very cold – but it was quiet, too. For the first time since leaving the beach, Anna felt like she she could properly hear her own thoughts. And she had so many of them! It was difficult to get them all straight, but Anna supposed there wasn't any rush. Now that she was dead, she had all the time in the world.

'Oh, good,' said a voice. 'You made it.'

Anna gasped. At once, water rushed into her mouth – but this time, her chest didn't hurt at all. With a growing sense of dread, Anna opened her eyes.

A school of fish was hovering beside her head. They scattered as she looked at them, darting away in flashes of yellow and red, gliding through the water as easily as birds in the wind. Great mounds of coral were heaped all around her, rising up in a mass of twisted shapes and lurid colours: they grew together as one, white spires merging with yellow sponges, orange tridents pushing through clouds of pink and blue. Strange scarlet trees spread their branches through the seabed, their ends wiggling like veins.

Had there been air in her lungs, the beauty of the reef might have taken Anna's breath away. But there was no air. Anna sucked down another mouthful of water, the salt prickling at her tongue. She was lying on her back on the ocean floor – but she was not dead. There was a nasty cut on her arm where Sylvie had bitten her, a wound that wept with black-coloured blood, but the injury didn't seem to be causing her any pain. Somehow, through some random miracle, she had survived Sylvie's attack – but how?

'It might take some getting used to,' said the voice. 'It's a very old spell, but it should last for an hour or two, so long as I did it properly.' There was a giggle. 'I've never kissed anyone before. Did it hurt?'

Anna scrambled backwards as Sylvie drifted out from behind a pillar of coral. The girl was smiling kindly, her eyes glowing with curiosity, but her skin was now as lucent as glass, so sheer that Anna could clearly see the skeleton moving inside. Her heart pounded with fear as Sylvie came towards her, swimming through the water in a tangle of hair and bones.

'What have you done to me?' she said, the words coming out in a burble.

Sylvie giggled again as she floated up to Anna's face.

'I gave you a gift,' she said. 'A mermaid's kiss. My sisters say the sailors used to beg for them as their ships were sinking, so they could see the other side of the ocean before they drowned. I don't think many of them ever did. We don't like humans coming down here.' She paused. 'Except for you, of course. You're not like the others. You're *fun*.'

She squeezed Anna's shoulder. Her touch was so chilling that Anna felt like her skin had been pinched between two icicles. She wanted to move away, but she forced herself to stay calm, drawing in another long, watery breath. Her lungs didn't feel like lungs anymore. What had Sylvie's spell done to her insides?

'You should move around a bit,' said Sylvie. 'You'll feel better once you do. The kiss won't do anything about the cold. If you don't get your blood pumping, you might freeze.'

The thought of her blood freezing was enough to make Anna leap off the seabed in fright. She paddled around the coral court, trying to avoid the sharp, spiky edges, sending schools of tiny fish fleeing across the reef. As she swam, she caught glimpses of other animals hidden away in cracks and crevices: crabs and eels lurking in hidden holes, as well as the shadows of much larger things, swimming low through the deepest channels. With a nervous kick, Anna returned to Sylvie's side.

But she didn't feel as afraid as she had before. Anna had always been a strong swimmer, but now she was swimming faster than ever, slicing through the ocean with ease. Each new breath of water seemed to fill her with energy, powering her muscles in an instant, always ready to fuel her next stroke. She laughed as she spiralled past a great rainbow-coloured tower, delighting in the fantastic colours, in the shapes that seemed to be carved out from a dream. She didn't want to admit it, but now that she knew she wasn't dying, Sylvie's gift was actually rather wonderful.

'Good,' said Sylvie. 'I think you're ready to go a little deeper. Follow me, and stay close, *Anna*.' Her eyes sparkled. 'But be careful. There might be sharks about.'

10

A NERVOUS WRECK

THE REEF WAS MUCH LARGER THAN ANNA HAD first thought. The outcrop where she had woken up had been relatively close to the surface; now she was far below it, the pressure in her ears tightening as she dropped to new depths. Flowing strands of seaweed brushed against her arms and legs as Sylvie led her through the coral mass, slithering through holes and squeezing under ledges, following fish of all colours as they twisted and teemed through the cold, dark sea.

'Not long now,' called Sylvie. 'The shipwreck is just up ahead.'

She wriggled through a narrow gap, her ribcage glimmering in the dim ocean light. Anna had begun to notice that the further underwater they travelled, the less Sylvie looked like a human girl. When Sylvie grabbed onto a handhold, the bones in her hand seemed to disappear, allowing her fingers to curl around the coral like the tentacles of an octopus. At other times, when she changed direction quickly, her translucent skin would shimmer and, for a moment, Anna was able to see the thousands of tiny scales covering her body. But the strangest things of all were her legs. Anna could see the two sets of bones stretching down to Sylvie's feet, and yet her legs always moved as one, sliding through the water like the tail of a serpent. Anna knew that mermaids were supposed to be half-human, half-fish, but Sylvie's body wasn't split as neatly as the pictures she had seen in her books. As she swam through the tangled reef, Sylvie seemed to have fishy features from head to toe.

'Has anyone else ever been this way?' said Anna. Her voice was still a burble, but she pressed on anyway. 'I mean, has anyone else ever visited the shipwreck?'

'Only once,' said Sylvie. 'Years ago, now. It was a surprise. I thought the humans had forgotten all about it. I thought it was mine.' She shrugged. 'She didn't see me. She never came back.'

Anna remembered the wetsuit and the oxygen tank in her bedroom cupboard. She pictured Madeleine Graves descending through the coral, pursuing her quest to the bottom of the ocean, bright eyes watching her from the shadows. Wasn't it terribly dangerous to go scuba diving without a partner? *When you dive alone, you die alone* – she had read that somewhere once, a long time ago.

Before, she had thought that she and Madeleine might have shared the same curiosity. Now she wondered if they shared the same recklessness as well.

'We're here,' said Sylvie.

She turned and swam down a coiling red path, the coral squiggling like a brain spilled down a staircase. Anna followed her around the bend – and gasped.

Resting on the ocean floor was a ship – an *enormous* ship, at least twenty metres long, its hull coated thickly with coral growths. Two great masts rose imposingly from the rotting wooden deck; the sails they had once carried were nowhere to be seen, lost to the water long ago. The lower deck seemed to have disintegrated entirely. A pair of cannons had broken out from the bowels of the boat, smashing their way through the waterlogged gunports; they lay side by side on the seabed, damaged beyond repair.

'We're here,' said Sylvie.

But at the front of the ship, some of the coral had been chipped away. Anna swam to the prow, sidling up beside the figurehead: a miniature lion, its paw raised in a soggy attack. She ran her hand over the place where the coral had been cleared, tracing the letters carved deep into the wood.

ZEEDUIVEL

'Isn't it nice?' said Sylvie. 'It'll all fall apart eventually, but I've done my best to preserve it. I had a word with the crabs and the shipworms – told them to leave it alone.' She smiled proudly. 'None of my sisters ever found it. I'm the only one who could have shown you the way.'

Anna was barely listening. She ran her fingers over the carved letters once more, lost in thought. Madeleine Graves had been here; had swum in this very spot, cleaning away the coral to confirm the identity of the sunken ship. Where had she gone next?

'Let's have a look around,' she burbled. 'I want to see the other side.'

Sylvie shrugged again, gliding away with a flick of her conjoined legs. Anna made her way more slowly around the hull, peering into the dark spaces where the wood had broken apart, wondering if she was brave enough to venture inside. Sylvie had said that she'd driven away the crabs and worms – but what about the sharks, sea snakes, and stingrays? Anna moved on quickly.

'You might like this,' called Sylvie. 'Seems like the sort of thing you're looking for.'

She was floating at the rear of the ship. Anna kicked her feet quickly to catch up, marvelling at the intricate details adorning the stern. Here, too, the coral had been cleaned away, revealing a line of fearsome wooden warriors, each one no bigger than a doll. They held swords and spears in their tiny hands, glaring out at the reef with mottled faces, gallantly trying to scare away any fish who might approach their vessel.

Between the warriors sat a row of three windows. There was no longer any glass in place, but each window remained covered by a metal grate, woven so finely that only the smallest animal could have wriggled between its bars. But the metal did not appear to be very secure. Someone – or something – had tried to prise the third grate aside, making a gap between the grate and the window frame. The gap didn't look big enough for an adult – but if she sucked in her stomach, and bent her arms just right, Anna thought that an eleven-year-old girl might just be able to squeeze through.

'This is rather new,' said Sylvie. She turned a lazy somersault in the water, her skin-scales glistening. 'I've never been into that room. The door is blocked on both sides.'

Anna hooked her fingers around the third

window grate, anchoring herself to the hull. From the size of the stern, and the extravagance of the carved wooden guards, she guessed that the room beyond the windows must be the grandest cabin of all – the captain's cabin, probably. What could be in there?

'Are you thinking about going in?' asked Sylvie. 'You *are* brave. I can stay here and keep watch, if you like. I'll make sure nothing sneaks in after you.'

It sounded like a challenge. In truth, Anna wasn't sure what she was thinking. She had wanted to learn more about the lost shipwreck, but never in a million years had she imagined that she might be seeing it with her own eyes, let alone going in-side. The whole adventure sounded too dangerous to comprehend – and yet here she was, swimming through the sea like a human fish, the wreck of the *Zeeduivel* stretched out before her.

Only a child could fit through that window. This

was her chance to explore the ship like Madeleine never could.

'Okay,' she said. 'I'll just go in for a minute. I'll yell if I need you, all right?'

Sylvie nodded. Anna took a deep breath, raising her legs and guiding her feet into the hole. The edges of the grate were jagged and sharp, but she avoided them as best she could, arching her back as she slid her body through. As she twisted her head, Anna caught sight of Sylvie's face, an ominous glow of twinkling eyes and wild hair; and then her head popped through the hole, and she was inside.

The water in the cabin was icy cold. Anna grabbed onto the window frame, scared to let her feet touch the unseen floor. Rays of murky ocean light were filtering through the rotting deck, but they weren't enough to see by. Anna blinked hard, hoping that Sylvie's 'kiss' might have improved her vision as well. She was beginning to see the edges of things: odd shapes poking out from the gloom, sinister and strange. She flinched away from something that turned out to be an upturned chair; she was startled again by a lantern on a chain, still hanging from the cabin roof, its stillness disturbed by her presence. More broken furniture was piled up by the door, battered and shattered by the ship's crash into the sea. Sylvie had not been lying. There was no other way in.

'How is it?' called Sylvie. Her voice sounded very far away. 'Do you need any help?'

'Not yet,' said Anna. 'Thanks, though.'

Her eyes were adjusting properly now. Shiny things were glinting on the cabin floor, hidden among the debris: candlesticks and bottles, barrel rings and china plates. None of them looked particularly valuable. Anna drifted boldly into the centre of the cabin, scrutinising every shadow. Why had Madeleine Graves been so fascinated by this ship?

A long, thin object caught her eye, nestled in the rubble beneath the broken window. Anna shivered as she sank down towards it, her teeth chattering loudly. With a sudden thought, she reached down to squeeze the hilt of her knife, looking forward to a burst of magical warmth.

But the knife was not there.

Anna froze. She patted her side again, sure she had made a mistake. But her scabbard was empty. The knife was gone.

A great clunk echoed out from above Anna's head. She looked up just as the window grate snapped closed, bent by some unknown force. She darted up as fast as she could, staring out of the wreck with panicked eyes, her heart thrashing with terror.

Sylvie was floating calmly outside the window. In one hand she held an iron cannonball, the metal still ringing from its collision against the grate.

She smiled as Anna screamed, baring all of her sharp, piranha-like teeth, laughing as her black hair swirled in the sea.

In her other hand she held the white knife.

11

DEAD MAN'S CHEST

'GIVE IT BACK!' SCREAMED ANNA. 'LET ME OUT this instant!'

Sylvie twirled the knife around her fingers, her eyes shining even brighter than the blade.

'No,' she said. 'I don't think so. This isn't a toy for a *human* to play with.' She twirled the knife again. 'And it looks much better in my hand, don't you think?'

Anna grabbed onto the metal grate, pushing

against it with all her strength. It didn't move. She screamed again as Sylvie let the cannonball fall idly from her hand, the iron sinking quickly to the ocean floor.

'It's a shame, really,' said Sylvie. 'I *have* enjoyed being your friend. My sisters don't ever play with me anymore, and you're so much more fun than they are. But they also told me that humans can't be trusted. They say you're *greedy*. They say you're *selfish*.' She pouted. 'We only ever had one proper treasure, and we shared it with the humans centuries ago, as a kindness. But the humans wasted it. They kept it for themselves, instead of doing what we told them.' Sylvie paused to admire the knife again, smiling at the sparkling blade. 'I don't think it would be wise to share *this* treasure. I think I'll keep it for myself – so I might just have to leave you here forever.'

Anna howled. She kicked and scratched at the

side of the ship as ferociously as she could, trying to break through; but although the wood was old and swollen, it did not bend to her attacks. Anna sank back into the cabin, panting.

'You're not my friend,' she spat. 'You were *never* my friend. You used my own name against me – to lure me here against my will. You're no better than any of the other monsters.'

She punched the metal grate in frustration, wincing as a haze of blood floated out from her knuckles. Sylvie swam forward until her face filled the window, her eyes glowing like fog lamps. She looked rather hurt.

'I didn't force you to do anything,' she said defensively. 'You wanted to come and explore the ship, and you wanted to send away the dead boy as well. I only prodded you in the right direction.' Her eyes flickered. 'In the old wood, I could use your name to control you like a puppet. But the spell's not as powerful here. You're already learning to fight it off.'

She said the last part kindly, as if she was trying to make Anna feel better about the situation. Anna glared back at her, sticking up her fingers in the rudest gesture she could think of. Now that she was trapped, she was thinking urgently about another spell – the mermaid's kiss that Sylvie had planted on her arm. How much longer would it last? Anna took another breath, trembling as the water rushed into her lungs. How long did she have before her next breath drowned her instead?

'I'm sorry,' said Sylvie. 'I wish there was another way. I promise I won't forget you. I'll always carry a piece of you with me, wherever I go.'

She pointed to her silvery necklace. Anna stared closely at the needles – and then, with a shudder of recognition, she realised they weren't needles at all. Thousands of tiny fish bones had been threaded together around Sylvie's neck, shimmering wickedly across her breast. Sylvie skimmed a finger along the bones, smiling proudly.

'I collected all of these myself,' she said. 'But my sisters say that human bone shines the brightest. I should rather like to wear some bones as bright as that.' She stared hungrily at Anna. 'I bet your bones will be the most beautiful of all.'

Anna felt her body go numb with fear. She tried to speak – to plead, to protest – but no words came. She didn't want to be a necklace. She didn't want to be anything. All she'd wanted to do was explore the shipwreck – and now that one desire had sealed her fate. She let out a wretched sob, invisible tears leaking out into the sea.

To her surprise, Sylvie looked rather glum as well. The fairy girl turned away from the window for a long moment, her shoulders slumped, her wild hair tossing back and forth. Then she looked back with a new determination, her sharp face set in a frown.

'I shan't stay to watch you die,' she said. 'I'll only come back once the fish have picked you clean. But I won't leave you alone either – you're too tricky for that. I'll have to introduce you to someone new.'

She raised her arm with a mighty swoosh, the stolen knife glinting as it sliced through the water. Sylvie pointed the blade quickly at the reef, her eyes focusing on some unseen thing. The tip of the white knife began to sparkle.

'Come here,' said Sylvie softly. 'I've got a job for you.'

She twirled the knife again, pointing it through the window frame. Anna shrank back as a great shadow passed over the top of the wreck, blocking all light from view. She began to shake as a new face appeared at the window grate, staring in at her with a very toothy smile.

'Don't look so surprised,' said Sylvie. 'I told you there were sharks about.'

Anna whimpered as she stared back at the shark. She knew it was a real animal – knew she had seen its picture in her schoolbooks – but there, in that horrible moment, she was convinced the beast had swum directly out of her nightmares. The shark's gums were pink and bloody, as if fresh from the hunt; its teeth were perfect triangles, enormous and sharp. Its back was grey, but its belly was pale and white, wide enough to stomach Anna's entire family. Its small black eyes shone with a wicked intelligence, hungrily watching Anna's every move.

Sylvie pointed the knife directly at the shark's long grey snout.

'I want you to guard this human for me,' she said. 'Make sure she doesn't find a way to escape. Don't leave until she … stops moving.'

The shark lowered its head. Sylvie smiled sadly,

stroking the shark affectionately along the tail, running her fingers over its wide, curving fins.

'Goodbye,' she said quietly. 'It was nice to know you, Anna.'

And then she turned and swam away, a skeleton gliding through the water, vanishing in a flurry of bones.

Once upon a time, on a holiday taken when she was very, very young, Anna had decided to go for a swim, all by herself. Her family were staying at a friend's house, and the friend owned a pool; and so, on a lovely sunny day, with the birds singing sweetly in the trees, and with nobody else around, Anna dragged a chair over to the pool fence and unhooked the gate with a flick of her fingers. At first, she had only felt brave enough to dip her feet in the shallow end, sighing with happiness as the water cooled her toes; but as the minutes ticked past, Anna had begun to feel bolder, setting her sights on the deep end where only the adults could go. She found a pool ring, tucking it snugly around her tiny body, and then set off from the side, paddling bravely into unchartered waters.

And then, when the deep water was all around her, when her feet could no longer touch the bottom, she had let go of the pool ring by mistake, and slipped right through the middle.

Standing on the floor of the pool, her head underwater, desperately holding on to the last breath in her lungs, Anna had understood what a serious mistake she had made. Time had seemed to split in two, neatly dividing into the happiness of *then* and the horror of *now*. She had clenched her fists tight, hoping and wishing that the clock would reverse itself, that the seconds would tick back to that time when nothing had gone wrong.

And it had worked. The Professor had crashed into the pool beside her, still fully dressed in his jacket, shirt and pants; he had dived to her side and pulled her to the surface, lifting her back into the warm, sunny air. And Anna had cried and cried, and she had kept on crying until someone had given her an ice-cream cone, and when she had finally calmed down she had promised to never go swimming by herself ever again.

Anna remembered all of this as she sat alone in the shipwrecked cabin, watching the shark swim back and forth. She clenched her fists together, hoping that someone would realise where she was, wishing that someone would come to her rescue. No-one did.

This time, she would have to save herself.

The shark pressed its nose against the window

147

grate as Anna swam back into the shadows. She pressed her hand against every wooden panel, searching for any weakness. Each panel was soft under her touch, but never quite soft enough; Anna tried to pull the weakest panel away to no avail. She moved her attention to the roof instead, rolling over in the water to kick her feet against the upper deck. Those planks were softer – but as she pressed against the boards, the shark's great shadow swooped overhead, sending her scrabbling to the floor in fright. Even if she did escape the wreck, how could she fight the shark without her knife? She needed to find another weapon.

Anna swam down to the corner beside the window, remembering the long object she had seen before the window grate had snapped shut. The *Zeeduivel* had been equipped with cannons: might the sailors have carried swords as well? She reached into the darkness, daring to hope.

It was a crowbar. Anna cleaned off the grime, staring in disbelief at the bright yellow hook. The crowbar looked new – nowhere near four hundred years old. She raised the bar to her face, squinting at the words written on the handle.

PROPERTY OF M. GRAVES.

'Yes!' yelled Anna. She swung the crowbar with delight. 'Thank you, Madeleine!'

Suddenly it all made sense. It was Madeleine Graves who had tried to pry the window grate aside – but Madeleine had dropped her crowbar before the hole was wide enough, losing the tool inside the ship. Had she meant to come back for it? Anna hooked the crowbar beneath a panel, grinning as the wood snapped easily under the pressure. Now she'd be able to break out of the wreck for sure.

But it still wouldn't be enough to defeat a shark.

Anna floated back to the pile of broken furniture, using the crowbar to lift away the smaller fragments. She needed to find something light and sharp – something she could drive into the shark's eyes if it came charging towards her. Anna tried not to imagine how it would feel to have the shark's colossal jaws close around her leg. She knew she was fighting a losing battle – knew Sylvie had probably succeeded in trapping her for good – but with Madeleine's crowbar in her hand, she had found a spark of hope. She pushed aside a broken chair, hunting through the pile.

There was a loud *clunk* as the crowbar struck something solid. Anna groaned. She really didn't have time for any more obstacles. She sank swiftly down to the ground, using her hands to clear away the debris, trying to see what she had hit.

'Oh,' she burbled. 'What's this?'

Sitting on the cabin floor was a large wooden chest. Anna ran her hands over the lid in surprise, wiping away the coating of ocean sludge. It was a wide, heavy-looking box, fastened at the front with a huge iron lock, the wood so old and waterlogged that it almost appeared black. Ornate metal bands ran around its edges, valiantly holding the box together after centuries undersea, but the wood had already begun to collapse, the slats falling inward to crush whatever was inside. Anna tugged on the heavy lock. Was this the treasure Madeleine had been searching for?

BANG!

Anna almost jumped out of her skin. She whirled around to see the shark smash its body against the window again, furiously gnashing its teeth. With a jolt of shock, Anna realised that its bulging eyes were fixed on the newly-uncovered chest. She scrambled away as the side of the ship began to creak, the boards finally crumbling under the shark's powerful attack.

Something was very wrong. Anna held up the

crowbar, unable to stop shaking as the shark rumbled against the hull. Sylvie had told the shark to guard her, not attack her – so what had changed? Anna racked her brain for clues, trying to remember Sylvie's exact words. *Make sure she doesn't find a way to escape* – had that been it? Anna dove back to the chest, tugging on the lock with all her strength. If the shark was trying to get in and stop her, then she must be closer to escaping than she had realised. But what could the chest possibly contain? A tunnel? A submarine? A harpoon gun?

The side of the ship burst open. Anna squealed as the shark knifed between the snapping planks, its tail thrashing, its jaws open wide: she smashed her crowbar down onto the chest, knocking a hole right through the lid. With a final burst of adrenaline, she thrust her hand into the box, desperately trying to grab the treasure within.

And then the cabin exploded with light.

12

FIGHT OR FLIGHT

THE LIGHT FROM THE CHEST WAS BLINDING. Anna screwed her eyes shut, scrambling away from the shark, terrified that its jaws might already be closing around her head. There was something in her hand – something smooth – something *weird*. She stumbled back through shards of furniture, squealing as splinters dug into her toes. The lights flashing behind her eyelids were as vivid as the coral outside. With a tremendous effort, she forced herself to look at the object in her palm.

She was holding a stone – a gemstone the size of a chicken egg, shining with every colour imaginable. All the colours of the rainbow were there, chips of red and purple intersecting with slivers of blue, gold, and green, but there were other colours too, colours that Anna had never seen before: the fiery glow of children dancing; the ebb of a lost love, deeper than black; the ultra-violet gleam of a thought passing through a mind. The colours singed Anna's eyeballs, and her palm as well; a great welt was forming on her skin, as if her cells themselves were rejecting the impossible light. But Anna couldn't let go of the stone. The gem was so beautiful, so full of possibilities, that all she wanted to do was stare at it forever – *but no*, said her brain, *there is danger nearby* – marvelling at the endless worlds contained within – *grey fins, white teeth, coming closer* – spoiling herself with the opulence, the splendour – *you are going to die* ...

Anna tore her eyes away. Feeling rushed back into her body: she gasped, crying out in agony, suddenly aware of a terrible pain in her leg. She spun around in the water, raising the crowbar above her head, the hooked end ready to strike.

But the shark was no longer moving. It had squeezed its entire body into the cabin, its fins tickling at the side of the chest, but now it was completely frozen, its black eyes fixed on the shining stone. For the first time since it had appeared by the wreck, the creature looked peaceful. With the corners of its mouth curling up, it almost looked like it was smiling.

Except ...

Anna swallowed back a scream, trying to keep very, very still. The shark was so distracted that its mouth had lolled wide open – and inside the shark's mouth, there was a foot. *Her* foot. A single white fang was piercing her ankle, sunk so deep into her flesh that it was locking her leg in place. Blood seeped thickly from the wound, streaming out around the shark's grey head.

The shark's nostrils twitched.

'Oh, no,' whispered Anna. 'Don't do that.' She quickly held up the strange stone, averting her own eyes from the light. 'You don't smell anything. Just keep – *ah* – looking over here …'

The opal-stone was hurting her palm – but Anna knew she couldn't afford to let go of it now. Slowly, carefully, she reached down with the crowbar, gently using the bar to lift up her leg. A cloud of blood erupted from the gash as she slid her foot free.

The shark quivered.

It was now or never. With a sudden burst of courage, Anna twisted around and kicked against the cabin wall, shooting swiftly through the water. She stuck the shining stone close to the shark's eye as she passed it, hoping to dazzle it for a few seconds more; and then she was ducking under the creature's fins, squeezing herself between the monstrous body and the broken planks, wiggling frantically to freedom. The shark rolled sluggishly as she fought her way past its tail fin, pushing against the scales, scrabbling over the final curve – *and then she was free*, swimming outside into the wide blue ocean.

But she wasn't safe yet. On their journey to the wreck, Sylvie had swum through the reef like a delicate fish, darting from rock to rock. Anna swam away from it like a maniac, kicking as hard as she could, blood streaming from her ankle. She glanced frantically over her shoulder as she climbed towards the surface, observing from the outside the shattered stern of the *Zeeduivel*. How long did she have before the shark pursued her? To her horror, she saw other dark shapes swimming through the reef, stalking her from beneath as she sped over the coral. Anna flinched as a new black fin emerged from behind a shelf; she wheeled around and changed direction as a sharp grey snout slid through a wash of seaweed. Suddenly the reef was alive with sleek grey bodies, sharks gliding out from every nook and cranny, a teeming mass of dark eyes and white teeth.

All of them were staring at the stone.

What had she found? Anna peeked daringly at the opal-stone as she sped through the reef, making her way towards the tallest coral tower. She had been told that the white knife was not an object from her world; *this*, surely, was another such item. The light flashing from the stone was brighter than the stars, more dizzying than a kaleidoscope, painting the sharks with lush greens and fizzing pinks. All of the sharks were snarling, their jaws opened wide, but they swam as if in slow motion, unable to get too close to the radiant colour.

But some of the beasts were getting bolder. Anna cried out as a hammerhead shark rose up from the pack, its bizarre face twisting towards her; she knocked it off course with a swing of the stone, shooting out a dazzling streak of light. Each breath she took was starting to feel tighter and tighter. There was a new tickling sensation in her nose, as if her body was finally realising that there was water in places where water shouldn't be. Her chest gave an awful shudder as she climbed up the side of a familiar coral pillar, dropping the crowbar behind her, using her free hand to pull herself up the craggy heights. A shark with tiger stripes nipped at her heels as she ascended the final steps; with a huge final push, Anna burst back above the surface, clambering atop the shelf where Sylvie had first dropped her so very long ago.

Anna vomited. She collapsed on the ocean

seat, coral digging into her stomach, vomiting out shower after shower of dirty, bloody water. Air rushed down her throat, inflating her lungs for what felt like the very first time: Anna screamed, scratching at her chest, trying to make the horrible pain go away. Everything hurt. Her insides were heaving; her legs were cut and bruised; *and her hand was on fire*, still holding the opal-stone, its surface blazing brighter than the afternoon sun. With a gasp of pain, Anna dropped the stone onto the shelf, staring down in fright as her toes were lit up with watery rainbows. Was this what Madeleine Graves had been searching for? Had Madeleine really been looking for a treasure from another world? Anna moaned as she dipped her scorched palm into the ocean, trying to soothe the angry red skin.

She hadn't thought this far ahead. The terrible shipwreck was beneath her, rotting in the deep – but dark fins were swirling all around the reef shelf, and dry land was still far from sight. There was no way out.

Anna slumped with exhaustion, rain and sea spraying against her face. She couldn't swim any further. As soon as a shark gathered up the courage to snatch her off the shelf, her life would be over.

At least she wouldn't end up as a necklace. Anna curled up on the shelf, wondering why Madeleine had never returned to the reef. Had she been eaten by sharks as well? Or had she decided that exploring the wreck again wasn't worth the risk? Anna hoped the scholar had survived. She imagined a face for Madeleine, kindly and wise: imagined her smiling, safe and sound on the other side of the world, reading a dusty old book with the same wild enthusiasm as the Professor.

If she thought about it hard enough, she could almost believe it was true.

A colossal fin sailed past her arm. Anna

snatched up the stone at her feet, shining the colours through the water. The dark shapes recoiled for a moment, but returned almost at once, finally brave enough to approach the rainbow light. Anna spun around, shooting beams in as many directions as she could, but there were too many sharks: too many fins, too many eyes, too many teeth. This was it – the final stand – the end of all her adventures.

'Hey! Anna! Need a lift?'

Anna almost fell off the shelf in shock. Another dark shape was flying towards her – a shape with a voice, arcing down from the clouds. She reached out just as a shark leapt hungrily from the water; she gasped as another hand met her own, hauling her out of the sea and into the sky, pulling her onto a piece of carpet that was speckled with silver stars.

'Gotcha!' cried Max. He pumped his fist in delight, the wind blowing through his tufty hair. 'I *knew* we'd find you!'

'Gotcha!' cried Max.

Anna held on for dear life as the magic carpet skimmed over the waves. Sharks twisted and roiled below, smashing their bodies against the water, furious that their prey had escaped them. Anna's mind was fuzzy with relief. She knew she had a hundred things to say to Max – a thousand things, maybe – but, for now, a single question popped from her lips.

'*We?*' she said. 'What do you mean, *we?*'

She jumped as something nudged against her neck. Electric blue whiskers tickled her cheeks as she looked down in astonishment, staring into a pair of bright yellow eyes.

Max grinned. 'You'd better strap yourself in,' he said, stroking the cat. 'We've got a *lot* to talk about.'

13

A WELL-SPUN TALE

THE STORM CRACKLED ALL AROUND THEM AS THE carpet flew back across the sea. Max knelt bravely at the prow, his tiny English-Persian dictionary clutched tightly in his hands, whispering softly to the carpet as it swerved around the waves. Anna lay back as best she could, her body tired beyond belief, the wondrous jewel glittering on the carpet beside her.

'She arrived just after I got back to the house,' called Max, nodding at the cat. 'So I knew something bad must be happening. But then she just kept meowing and scratching against the door, like I hadn't got the message. It was driving Dad mental – he thought I'd let in a stray.' He frowned. 'Then she saw that picture of the spider, and she really went wild. She ran into my room and pulled the carpet out of my bag, all by herself. I think she would've flown off without me if I hadn't hurried up.'

Anna smiled, tickling the little cat under its chin. It tilted its head back, letting her scratch its chest, although it seemed reluctant to purr. With the rain falling on its head, and the carpet whooshing along at top speed, she doubted the cat was having much fun.

'So we knew you were in trouble, but we didn't know where to look,' continued Max. 'We've just been circling around for the last hour. Which seemed safe enough in a ghost town, as long as we didn't get hit by lightning. But then we saw your light, and we came as quickly as we could.' He glanced back at the glowing stone, his eyes wide. 'Where did you find *that?*'

Anna groaned. 'It's a long story,' she said. 'A long, horrible story. I still don't understand how it's going to end. This town is weird, Max – really, really weird.'

She ran her hand through the cat's soft, wet fur. Soon, she would tell Max everything – about the sharks and the shipwreck, the spider and Sylvie – but for now, all of that could wait. Anna got onto her knees and crawled to Max's side, sliding her arms around her brother and squeezing him tight.

'I'm sorry,' she said. 'I've been awful. I shouldn't have treated you like that. And what I said on the beach – I didn't – I mean, that wasn't ...'

Max sniffed.

'It's all right,' he said. 'I could tell that friend of yours was no good. I know you didn't mean it.' He turned his head, awkwardly meeting Anna's eye. 'And I'm sorry too. For what happened at my birthday. I wasn't really going to show anyone the carpet – or at least, I didn't think I was going to. But then ...' He trailed off for a moment, scrunching up his face. 'It's just, we've been having all these horrible adventures, and none of my old friends know anything about it. They don't know how much I've changed. They can't even see this.' He held up his dead hand, sadly wiggling his fingers. 'I just feel so different now, and I can't talk to anyone about it. And so, on my birthday, when all my friends were there in the same room as the carpet, I just got ... carried away.'

Anna thought about her meeting with Sylvie on the beach. With a spasm of guilt, she remembered how readily she had spilled her own secrets, all to a girl she barely knew. She wasn't any better than Max – in fact, she was *worse* than Max. Anna squeezed her brother tighter, wishing she could take back every mean thing she'd done to him. Soaring across the ocean, holding Max close, she suddenly realised there was no-one in the world who she would rather go on an adventure with. After all they had been through together, Max was truly her best friend.

And that meant she would have to tell him everything.

'I lost the knife,' she blurted. 'Sylvie took it from me. The mermaid girl. She took it and it's gone. I don't know how to get it back.'

Max's arms stiffened. Anna looked away, feeling utterly ashamed. She reached out to stroke the cat again, hoping it might comfort her, but the cat looked alarmed by the news as well. It whipped its tail back and forth against the carpet, its golden eyes even wider than usual.

'And the spider?' said Max. 'Is Dad's story true? Have you seen it?'

Anna nodded. She could feel the events of the past two days welling up inside her: a terrifying jumble of chases, death traps and betrayals, each one more frightening than the next. As Max piloted the carpet down to the stormy beach, Anna finally let the entire story spill out. By the time the carpet had come to rest on the sand, Max's face had turned white as a sheet.

'... and so that's why Madeleine Graves came to Mermaid's Purse in the first place,' finished Anna. 'To find an old shipwreck, lost for hundreds of years. She must have known there was treasure inside. The only thing I don't know is whether Madeleine realised the spider was real, and whether or not she – *ah*.'

Her ankle buckled in pain as she stepped onto the beach, the cut from the shark tooth still dribbling with blood. Max gasped as he noticed the wound for the first time. He pulled a handkerchief from his pocket, leaning over to press it against Anna's foot. Anna winced as the fabric sank into the wound, stemming the blood flow.

'I hope you haven't blown your nose on that,' she muttered.

Max grinned. Anna flinched as the little black cat jumped up onto her shoulder, pressing its nose against her neck with a rumbling purr. She shivered as its whiskers brushed against her skin, sending a strange tingling sensation all through her body. For the first time that day, her thoughts felt clear.

'We need to get back to the house,' she said decisively. 'Madeleine Graves might have understood what was going on in this weirdo town, but I sure don't. We need to see if she wrote down anything else – and especially see if she recorded anything about *this*.'

She pointed at the stone. The gem was still glowing, but the vibrant colours had begun to dim against the deep blue of the carpet. Anna leant cautiously over the stone, only looking at it out of the corner of her eye. How long had it sat dormant before she touched it? The hand she had held it with felt completely raw, as if she had been swinging on monkey bars for far too long. Could she bear to pick it up again?

The cat meowed. It leapt off Anna's shoulder, snatching the bloody handkerchief away from her ankle. Then it ran over to the gem and dropped the hanky neatly on top, flipping the whole thing over with its paws. The children watched in surprise as it gathered the four ends of the handkerchief together and picked them up in its tiny mouth, the gemstone swinging neatly in the bloodstained bundle.

'Hey,' said Max indignantly. 'We were using that.'

But Anna's ankle was no longer bleeding. Anna poked tentatively at the newly formed scab, her skin still buzzing with an electric tingle. She smiled at the cat, patting it on the head.

'Thanks,' she said. 'That feels much better.' She slowly stood up and walked gingerly across the beach. To her relief, her coat and scarf were sitting nearby, right where she had left them – or rather, where Sylvie had forced her to leave them. Anna shrugged the raincoat over her shoulders, shuddering as it pressed against her sea-soaked clothes. Suddenly all she wanted was to get home to the fire.

'We'll have to walk from here,' said Max apologetically. He rolled up the carpet and tucked it under his arm, leading the way between the sand dunes. 'Dad's been a lot more alert since he got trapped in that boat in Iran. I told him I was only going out to get rid of the cat, but that was an hour ago now – and he was already cross that you were still gone. If we don't come up with a good excuse, this might be our last adventure for a while.'

Anna nodded to herself, wearily scanning the hills for the spider as she dragged along her sore foot. She was still trying to put everything in order. Madeleine Graves had been drawn to Mermaid's Purse because of a story: a message in a bottle, thrown overboard four centuries ago. The story had been about a spider – a huge, monstrous spider – and, for the most part, the story seemed to be true. It had been written by a group of sailors, who had likely encountered the spider when they went ashore, but their ship had been wrecked as they tried to sail away, sinking to the bottom of the reef. And inside their ship, there was ...

Anna paused, a thought pricking at the back of her head. What exactly had the Professor said when he was telling them the story? She stared out at the horizon, chewing on her lip. To her mild surprise, she found that she didn't recognise the hills around her. Max was leading them along a different route to the way she had come before, climbing down hills where she had climbed up them, weaving them back to town in a wiggling line.

Anna gasped as something sharp dug into her leg. The little black cat was pawing at her, sticking its claws into her flesh, its tail whipping with distress. A memory of another voice flew suddenly through Anna's mind – Sylvie's voice, dangerous and dark:

Some of her trapdoors are so well-hidden that not even I can see them.

'Max!' yelled Anna in alarm. 'Stop! I think we should go back –'

She recoiled as a bolt of lightning struck the hill-top beside her. Max spun around, his face scrunched up in concern – and then Anna was screaming as the earth exploded beside them, a great circle of dirt and webbing rising into the air. A pair of hairy legs grabbed Max by the shoulders, dragging him down into a hidden hole, a rope of webbing already strung around his chest – and then the flash of lightning passed, and the trapdoor was swinging shut, and Max was gone.

14

SEVERED TIES

ANNA SPRINTED UP THE HILLSIDE, HER EYES fixed on the closing trapdoor. The scab on her ankle tore open as she launched herself into the air; she gritted her teeth as she flew towards the trapdoor, bracing herself for impact.

Her feet never hit the ground.

Anna gasped as she tumbled beneath the earth, the massive trapdoor closing right behind her as she rolled down a long, round passageway lined with thick white webs. Some-where ahead of her, she could sense the great spider – could hear Max's screams – but as she fell, she had no control over which direction she went. New tunnels branched out around her; Anna stuck out her hand, rolling to the left, anxiously listening out for any sign of her brother. Had she turned the right way? With a sudden bump, she felt the ground level out beneath her.

'Max!' Anna staggered to her feet, spinning around in the darkness, her fists raised in front of her face. '*Max!* Say something!'

There was no reply. Anna stumbled through the webs that had caught around her legs; she stuck a hand out to steady herself, holding onto the tunnel wall. She frowned at the soft, tickly feeling beneath her fingers. Weren't webs usually sticky? She limped down the passage as fast as she was able, tripping through web after web, her ankle wet with blood.

There was a small *meow* at her side. Anna jumped, staring down in surprise at the little black cat, its golden eyes shining with a light of their own. Max's handkerchief was still clutched in its mouth, the rainbow stone glowing faintly from within.

'Thanks, kitty,' she panted, kneeling down. 'You're a good friend.' She took the handkerchief from its mouth. 'If we make it out of here alive, you can have all the sausages in the world.'

The cat purred. Anna leant against the furry wall, nervously wriggling her fingers. Her palm was still stinging, the tender skin feeling as if it had been stretched too tightly over her bones. But she didn't have a choice. If she was going to find the spider – if she was going to *fight* the spider – she was going to need a light.

She slipped her hand into the handkerchief, grabbing the gemstone, twisting her head away in anticipation.

A burst of rainbow light blazed through the tunnel. Anna pulled out the gem, her palm already burning, illuminating the webs around her feet with whirling arcs of red and gold – and then she was screaming, leaping away from the wall, shaking her arms and legs in absolute horror.

The tunnel walls were covered in spiders. Anna retched in revulsion as the spiders swarmed over each other, thousands of furry brown bodies climbing and scurrying over webs old and new. Worse still, they seemed to be drawn to the light. Anna tiptoed on the spot as a pair of spiders dropped from the roof, creeping across the tunnel floor, their tiny fangs poised to strike.

The cat pounced. In an instant, it trapped the first spider beneath its paws, swiftly impaling the little monster with its claws. The second spider wheeled quickly around, scurrying for the safety of the walls, but the cat moved even faster, leaping across the tunnel and pressing its face against the spider's back. Anna looked away as the cat chomped down, the spider wriggling frantically as its abdomen was bitten in two.

'Yuck,' she muttered. 'Maybe you'll be too full for sausages, then.'

The cat looked up at her proudly, a pair of legs protruding from its mouth. Anna grimaced as she hurried past, holding the gemstone out like a lantern, trying not to look at the awful bodies teeming above her head.

Fortunately, the cat's attack seemed to have made the rest of the spiders wary. They kept their distance as Anna rushed down another passage, twisting and turning through the labyrinth. She didn't know if she was heading in the right direction, but she chose the lower path whenever she could, hobbling down into the depths of the earth. Hadn't the Professor said the spider had come from deep underground? With a pang of regret, Anna pictured her father sitting beside the fireplace, looking fretfully at the door, his face creased with worry as the storm thundered down around the house. They had been close – *so close* – to making it home safely. They could have solved the rest of the mystery from the comfort of their beds, poring over Madeleine's old notebooks, trying to uncover why she had sought the secrets of the shipwreck with such vigour. The opal-stone would probably be valuable – in fact, it was almost certainly price-less – but if Madeleine really was anything like the Professor, she wouldn't have travelled to Australia for profit alone. So why had she come? Anna tried to piece it all together as she skidded around a corner, the black cat still running by her side.

She didn't see the hole in the tunnel floor until it was too late. Anna cried out in surprise as she began to fall again, her foot slipping directly through a thin covering of web. She covered her head with her arms as she bounced down a deep, dark shaft, squashing spiders by accident as her elbows smashed into the sides of the tunnel, whimpering as even more spiders fell down onto her coat, her hands, her face. How deep did the labyrinth go? Then the shaft was spitting her out the other end, and the cat was flying after her, and Anna was yelping in pain as her body collided with a stony floor.

She was lying in a chamber – a chamber with round, web-covered walls, its ceiling pockmarked with a series of enormous holes. In the centre of the chamber was a vast pool of water, its surface black and still; web-covered stalactites hung toothily from the roof above, their ends wet with cave dew, dripping sluggishly into the underground lake. The air was thick and musty. Anna wrinkled her nose as a smell wafted into her nostrils. It reminded her of the sour stench of a dead mouse in the wall, except much, much worse – more like a *thousand* dead mice, all trapped in the same wall together. With a growing sense of dread, Anna slowly sat up, holding the shining stone high above her head.

The walls of the chamber were lined with skeletons. They hung around the pool like a ring of macabre statues, their arms and legs wrapped in silken cocoons, their bodies still bearing the clothes and accoutrements they had worn in life. Anna whimpered as she backed away from a skeleton in a koala-print T-shirt, a dusty camera strapped around its neck; she turned and found herself face to face with a much older skeleton, its bones mottled and brown, a thin wooden spear still clutched in its decrepit hands. Anna jumped away, almost stumbling back into the pool. She forced herself to slow down, trying desperately to control her breathing.

A funny muffled sound echoed through the chamber. Anna spun around, holding up the stone like a shield of light, but the sound had come from the other side of the room, far across the water. Anna made her way cautiously around the edge of the pool, staring with morbid curiosity at each corpse she passed. How many people had the spider carried away? Anna winced as she brushed past a skeleton in a florescent pink swimsuit, its skull flashing her a toothy smile. She didn't smile back.

The cat ran ahead of her, padding delicately across the sticky floor. It stopped beside one of the smallest cocoons – a cocoon wrapped so thickly that no bones were showing at all. It meowed loudly, tapping its paw against the silken shell. Anna gasped as the cocoon began to shake.

'*Hewp!*' said the cocoon. '*Gep me owt uff heah!*'

The cat stood on its hind legs, scratching at the cocoon with its claws. Anna rushed to help, ripping apart the top of the cocoon, weeping with relief at the sight of the pale face within.

'*Help!*' yelled Max. He shook his head in a frenzied panic, staring wildly around the chamber. 'Is it gone? Did you kill it?' He spat out a mouthful of web, clicking his tongue in disgust. 'Why is it always me? Why can't *you* get dragged away by something for a change?'

Anna almost laughed. She tried her best to free Max's arms, pulling at the magic carpet that had been lashed to his chest.

'I haven't killed it,' she whispered. 'I don't know where it's gone. We need to be quiet, all right? Now that we've got the carpet, we might be able to fly out of here quicker than we came in.'

She glanced nervously at the holes in the ceiling. Was Max a good enough pilot to fly them back through the spider's tunnels? She could only hope.

'This place is *creepy*,' muttered Max. He looked sideways at the skeleton on his right. 'Why has the spider kept all of these, then? Are they *trophies?*'

Anna glanced at the nearest skeleton. With a spasm of shock, she realised it was the body that had hung on silken threads beneath the lonely tree, beckoning her across the hills towards its cold, dead embrace. Anna scowled as she stared up at the man in grey, longing to knock his skull from his stupid shoulders. Maybe the skeletons had started off as trophies, but the spider clearly knew how to use them as weapons as well.

Anna turned away – but to her surprise, the skeleton hanging on Max's other side also caught her eye. She peered curiously past the spidery shroud, trying to work out why the other body looked so familiar. A pair of spectacles hung limply from the skeleton's face, the cocoon of white webs blending easily with the long, grey hair still hanging from its skull. The body was dressed in a thick green coat, dusty and faded from its time beneath the ground.

But Anna still recognised the colour. She

frowned, brushing the dust from the lapel. She knew that coat. She had seen others exactly like it, hanging in a grimy wardrobe. Anna's heart skipped a beat. She didn't want to be right – didn't want to admit it was true – but maybe all the coats the skeleton had owned had been that same striking shade of –

'Anna!' cried Max suddenly. '*Look out!*'

Anna whirled around in time to see something burst from the pool of water. She raised her fists in panic, the opal-stone gleaming in her hand, ready to grapple with a pair of curving, gigantic fangs – but no fangs came. Instead, Anna found herself squealing as a translucent hand closed around her bloody ankle, dragging her swiftly to the water's edge.

'*There* you are,' whispered a silky voice. 'I've been looking for you *everywhere*.'

Anna's blood ran cold as Sylvie's head emerged from the water, her smile wide and sharp, her blue eyes shining with delight.

15

BEYOND THE GRAVE

'GET AWAY FROM HER!' YELLED MAX FURIOUSLY. He struggled frantically against the cocoon. 'If you touch one hair on her head, I'll come down there and I'll – I'll –'

His shouts were muffled as his head became re-tangled in the web, filling his mouth with silk.

'Oh, hush,' said Sylvie. 'We're *friends*, aren't we, Anna? We've had the most fabulous adventures together.' She cast Max a scathing look. 'I wouldn't expect a dead boy like *you* to understand.'

Anna slapped Sylvie as hard as she could. To her horror, her hand crashed right through the girl's cheeks, making her pale skin ripple like water. Sylvie gasped, releasing her grip on Anna's leg. Anna scrambled away, falling against the cobwebbed wall, feeling as if she'd just plunged her hand into a bucket of ice. She quickly tucked the shining stone into her pocket, hoping that Sylvie hadn't seen the source of the light.

'You didn't have to do that,' said Sylvie sulkily. 'I only came to see if you needed any help. I already set off some vibrations on the other side of the maze so your brother wouldn't get eaten too quickly.' She rubbed her cheek. 'I was doing a *nice* thing.'

Anna shook her head in disbelief.

'You stole my knife,' she said, trying to keep her voice calm. 'You left me in a shipwreck to die, so you could wear my bones as a necklace. So, no, Sylvie – I wouldn't say you're my friend. You're actually more of an enemy.'

Sylvie looked down at the water. Anna frowned, trying to make out the girl's expression in the pool's reflection. She was worried Sylvie might be stalling, buying time to launch her next attack – but when the girl's reflection finally came into focus, Anna was surprised to see that Sylvie's great blue eyes had gone dim.

'I didn't mean to hurt you,' said Sylvie sadly. She gave a little sniff. 'I just got a bit carried away, that's all. As soon as I left you in the water, I knew I'd made a mistake. I came right back to free you – but you'd already gone! That's when I realised I wanted to be friends with you forever. It wouldn't be right, to drown a human as clever as you.' She smiled brightly. 'It's a bit like the spider and the blind man, isn't it? I'm from one world and you're from another, but we can be the best of friends just the same.'

She seemed to think she'd made a very good point. Anna glared at her, remembering how Sylvie had described Archie Silcock as the spider's pet. She looked pointedly at the gash on her arm where the mermaid had bitten her, trying to choose her next words carefully.

But Max spoke first. He swallowed down the ball of web in his mouth, coughing and choking, his face convulsing with indignation.

'You're a *psychopath!*' he spluttered. 'You're evil – wicked – crazy …' He racked his brain for more adjectives. 'Bad-tempered – really mean – and *utterly insane!*'

Sylvie waved her hand at him dismissively. Her attention was fixed solely on Anna, watching her hopefully, waiting eagerly to hear what her 'friend' might say. Anna glanced at the cat for support, trying to decide what she should do. The cat had nestled low to the ground ever since the mermaid had arrived – but even when Sylvie had grabbed her, it had not pounced. Did that mean Sylvie was no longer a threat? Anna groaned, her mind a mess of thoughts.

'Fine,' she said. 'You can stay. But I don't forgive you – not yet. We'll see how much help you really are.'

Sylvie beamed. Anna stood up shakily, her hand aching from where she'd held the shining stone. She didn't want to work with Sylvie – didn't even want to look at her – but the unfortunate truth was that right now, stranded at the bottom of the spider's lair, Anna simply couldn't afford to pick another fight. Everything Max had said about Sylvie was true – but if the mermaid girl could help them, even the tiniest bit, it might mean the difference between life and death. Her revenge would have to wait.

For now, there were other revelations to deal with.

Anna walked over to the skeleton in the lime green coat. She carefully removed the spectacles from its skull, her fingers trembling as she wiped the dust from the lenses. The skeleton swayed slightly. It wobbled on its strings, its head nodding gently as Anna bumped against its hand. Suddenly Anna felt incredibly sad.

'Oh,' said Sylvie. 'That's *her*, isn't it? The one who came down to the shipwreck. The one you've been chasing after.' She peered at the bones. 'She's been dead a *long* time.'

Anna replaced the spectacles. She stared into the empty eye sockets of the long-lost scholar, trying to project the face she had imagined onto the cold white skull. It didn't work. Despite everything Madeleine had known – despite everything she had uncovered – her journey to Mermaid's Purse had been too much. Madeleine was dead, her body taken by a spider, her secrets taken to the grave.

'I can't see,' said Max crossly. He squirmed in his cocoon, trying to swing around. 'Can someone *please* get me out of here?'

Sylvie pushed her hands through the pool, sending a wave of water into the air. Max squealed as the wave splashed against him, disintegrating the cocoon. He stumbled away in shock, the carpet clutched against his chest, shooting Sylvie his meanest look.

'Let's get out of here,' he said to Anna, unfurling the carpet. '*She* can make her own way home. I bet she's been in and out of here a million times.' He pointed at Sylvie. 'You're probably friends with the spider too, aren't you? I bet you're just trying to distract us until he gets back.'

Sylvie stared at Max coldly. 'It's a *she*, actually,' she said. 'And no, we're not friends. My sisters warned me never to swim down this channel. I only came because I heard your awful screaming.' She sniffed. 'The huntress will eat my family too, if she can catch us. My sisters tried to do something about it when they first arrived here, but the humans didn't follow our plan. Now the huntress gets to eat whatever she can find.'

The huntress. Anna pictured the note from her bedroom. Madeleine's research had been so thorough that she had even known the spider's title. She sighed, running her hands over the dusty coat one last time.

She was about to turn away when her fingers ran over a bump.

Anna frowned. She unbuttoned the coat, wincing as the skeleton's bony ribcage was revealed. There was something slender in the inside pocket.

It was a notebook.

Anna's eyes bulged. She flipped through the book, astounded to see page after page of the same neat handwriting, notes and diagrams squeezed into every margin – drawings of the spider, and the *Zeeduivel*, and the funny jagged coastline of Mermaid's Purse. Anna quickly turned to the last page, reading through Madeleine's final notes, her heart beating fast.

She could almost feel the lightbulb appearing above her head.

'I know how to break the curse!' she cried.

Max looked up in surprise as Anna jumped onto the carpet. The cat followed suit, cuddling up beside Anna's legs, digging its claws securely into the fabric. Anna clapped Max on the back, a fierce look upon her face.

'Get us out of here,' she said. 'We need to find the spider – but not down here. This'll only work if we can get to the surface.'

Max frowned in confusion, but Anna looked so determined that he didn't ask any questions. He quickly pulled out his dictionary and began to thumb through it, his eyes darting over several highlighted words. He stabbed his finger down onto an open page with a grin, taking his place at the carpet's prow.

'*Parvaʒ!*' he cried.

At once the carpet began to move. Anna steadied herself as it rose into the air, brushing against the skull of the man in grey. With a series of whispered words, Max guided it away from the wall, hovering confidently over the underground lake. He smiled smugly at the astonished look on Sylvie's face.

'You can come too, if you want,' said Anna, staring down at the mermaid girl. 'It's going to be a dangerous ride, but I'm sure you'll think it's quite an adventure. We're going to do some good in the world – to finish off something your sisters tried to do long ago. But if you want to come with us, it's going to cost you.' She narrowed her eyes. 'Give me back my knife. Right. Now.'

She hoped she sounded as menacing as she intended. She glowered at Sylvie as the mermaid pouted up at her, swishing her arms carelessly through the water. Then, with a dramatic sigh, Sylvie raised a hand to her head, running her fingers through her hair. When her hand emerged from the tangle, a new object was gleaming against her skin: something that sparkled in the darkness, its razor-sharp edge awash with light. Sylvie twirled the white knife around her fingers, holding the blade just out of Anna's reach.

'You have so many treasures already,' she said. 'You didn't tell me about the carpet, or the cat, or that shining thing in your pocket.' She tilted her head thoughtfully. 'If we were *really* friends, it wouldn't matter so much if I kept this one. I bet real friends share things with each other all the time.'

Anna gritted her teeth. Her knife was so close,

and yet still so far away. Should she dive off the carpet and try to grab it? The thought gave her chills. She was worried that Sylvie might use any sudden movements as an excuse to chop her fingers off.

'Anna?' said Max nervously. 'I think I saw something moving up there.'

Anna glanced up at the ceiling. The stalactites were still dripping, and the webs were still rustling, but the entrances to the tunnels remained mercifully clear. She turned back to Sylvie, holding out her hand.

'Last chance,' she said. 'I don't have time to argue. Be my friend or don't. Your call.'

Sylvie stuck out her lip. Slowly, hesitantly, she held out the knife, twirling it around until the leather handle was pointing towards the carpet. Anna reached down, watching Sylvie's face for any sign of betrayal. With a spark of hope, she stretched out her hand, her fingertips brushing against the hilt –

– and then Max was screaming, and the carpet was jerking away, and Sylvie's bright blue eyes were wide with horror as the spider erupted across the ceiling, its legs stretching all the way across the cavern. Anna fell back on the carpet as the monster loomed above them, hissing with displeasure, her fingers still clutching desperately for the knife she had left behind.

16

THE LAST HUNTRESS

MAX SWUNG THE CARPET AROUND, FLIPPING desperately through his dictionary. Anna held tightly onto the cat as the carpet charged towards the spider, bracing for impact, but Max swerved them away at the last second, screaming out a series of Persian words at the top of his lungs. The carpet dipped swiftly down, soaring over Sylvie's head as it circled the lake. Anna clutched the carpet as it looped around, hoping she wouldn't be sick.

The spider was watching them closely, its legs perfectly still, its fangs clicking gently. Anna lost sight of it for a second as the carpet arced around. When she saw it again, the spider was frozen once more – except now it was closer, its head further down the wall, its legs curled tight against its enormous body. The monster was moving in flashes, creeping towards them in tiny bursts, its long legs skittering so quickly that Anna's eyes couldn't keep up. *How could they escape the cavern now?*

Max was tearing pages from his dictionary, holding them between his teeth, desperately trying to string together a new sequence of commands. Anna stared around at the cobwebbed walls in despair, frantically trying to buy them some more time.

Her gaze fell on the mottled brown skeleton, strung up by webs that looked older than any other. She waved her hand at it as the carpet whizzed past.

'*Sylvie!*' she yelled. '*Throw me that spear!*'

She could see the mermaid hiding in the water, blinking fearfully from under her cloud of black hair. At the sound of Anna's voice, Sylvie stuck out her head, swimming swiftly towards the skeleton Anna had pointed at. She snatched the wooden spear out of the cobwebs, throwing it up as the carpet circled past; Anna caught it deftly, spinning the weapon around her head.

'Are you ready, Max?' she shouted. 'Tell me when!'

Max ripped another page from his book. A jumble of different words were assembled before him, each one trapped under a different finger. He spat out a final piece of dictionary, catching it under his thumb.

'Ready!' he yelled.

Anna pulled back her arm. The carpet soared around the cavern again, curving back towards the spot where the spider was perched, flying so close to the beast that Anna could have counted the hairs on its belly. Anna took a deep breath as the spider extended its feelers, its two front legs stretching high into the air, its hooked fangs glistening – and then she was throwing the spear, and the spider was recoiling in surprise, and Max was yelling a strange sentence as loudly as he could.

The carpet dropped. Anna shrieked as they fell through the air, sure that Max had said the wrong thing – but then Max was sticking out his arm, shouting Sylvie's name, and suddenly a new passenger was climbing aboard as the carpet swung upwards. Sylvie clutched onto Anna with an icy grip as they wheeled past the stalactites, the giant spider scuttling and hissing in their wake: and then they were soaring through a tunnel of cobwebs, bouncing off the walls as Max wrestled with his dictionary once more.

The spider scuttled and hissed in their wake.

'What's your plan?' he shouted. 'Where do we need to go?'

'Out!' yelled Anna. 'Anywhere outside will do!'

She swiftly opened Madeleine's notebook, frantically re-reading the last page by the light of the stone. Sylvie gasped at the sight of the jewel, her expression awestruck, but she remained silent as Anna scanned Madeleine's final entry.

The curse is real.

Until now, the huntress has tolerated my presence, taking little interest in my movements throughout town. Now she is hungry, engorged with rage. She will not allow me to reach the beach again.

I have tried my best to free her, but the food she so craves has eluded my grasp. They took it from her, though they knew not what they did; I write this in the knowledge that soon she will come for me instead. This cursed town, with its great unfinished tale, shall now become the ending of my own story.

To those who may come after me, I offer only this:
Leave this place quickly, lest she take you as well.

The last line was good advice – but Anna didn't intend to follow it. She squeezed the shining jewel tightly as the carpet careened along the tunnel, arcs of light blazing across her face, remembering in a daze what the Professor had said at the end of his translation.

This might be the tale of an event yet to come.

'Hold on!' shouted Max.

Anna held the notebook in front of her face as the carpet crashed into a veil of web, covering them all with sticky strands of silk. For one long second, it seemed as if they might be stuck; but then the carpet pushed through, and a hidden trapdoor lifted up, and then they were out in the open air, flying towards the storm clouds, the rain washing the last of the cobwebs away.

The spider burst out onto the hills behind them,

its front legs twitching with fury. It sprang into the sky after the carpet, its limbs spread out in a nightmare silhouette, venom spraying from its fangs. Max shouted another command, urging the carpet to dip; Anna ducked as they sailed beneath the venom, twisting past the monster's hairy abdomen. As soon as the spider landed, it jumped again, hissing and spitting, throwing its body out like a net. Anna screamed as a gargantuan leg curled through the air, hooking onto the back of the carpet. Max almost lost his balance as the carpet lurched backwards, hurtling towards the ground as the spider fell back to earth, its leg dragging them all to certain doom.

Sylvie swung the white knife. The blade snicked through the air, slicing the tip of the spider's leg clean off. She brandished the knife with relish as the carpet zoomed away over the ocean, the spider screeching on the dunes below.

'I *knew* I should be the one to hold onto this,' she said, twirling the knife elegantly around her fingers. 'Wasn't that grand?'

Anna rolled her eyes. She moved the cat from her lap, setting it down between Max's legs, the jewel in her hand flashing as she held her fist aloft. It was time to put her plan into action.

'I need you to fly back to the spider!' she said to Max. 'I need to get close to its mouth!'

Max scrunched up his face. With a reluctant groan, he leant down and whispered to the carpet, holding on tight as winds whipped against the fabric. As he steered them around, Anna carefully rose to her feet, riding the carpet like a surfboard, the sea spraying against her legs as they flew back across the waves.

The spider was waiting for them. It had climbed to the top of the lighthouse, its legs curled up against the tower, skulking, lurking, readying itself for another leap. Anna stretched out her hand as the carpet soared towards the beast, her palm ablaze with colour and pain. Would the monster play along? Would her aim be true? It didn't matter now. It was too late to turn back.

The spider leapt into the air, its fangs clacking with fury, and Anna threw the gemstone into its open mouth.

The spider choked. It fell back to the earth, feelers scrabbling at its mouth, a horrible gurgling echoing from its throat. The children watched from above as it spun around on the ground, its legs spasming and snapping, its abdomen dragging a deep furrow through the sand. Its black eyes flashed with every colour of the rainbow, a carnival of fairy lights emanating from its skull.

And then the spider began to grow.

'Take us up!' screamed Anna. 'We need to get out of here!'

Max didn't have to be told twice. He pulled on the carpet, shouting new instructions, the wind spilling through his hair as the carpet blasted up towards the heavens. The cat yowled in panic; Sylvie let out a strange, wild sound, somewhere between a laugh and a cry. Anna looked over her shoulder as the spider swelled beneath them, its legs thickening, its abdomen bulging; she gasped as its fearsome head turned towards the sky, a beacon of light shooting from its maw.

It had started with a story. Anna closed her eyes as the light washed over her, centuries of history playing through her mind. Four hundred years ago, or maybe even earlier, a spider had emerged from underground, hungry and alone. It had feasted on the land, gorging itself on whatever it could find – and then, just as the Professor had told them, the spider had been supposed to eat stone. But not just any stone. The spider's final meal was destined to be a magical stone, a stone pulsing with power – a stone that would end its life.

But the stone had not been eaten. Anna pictured the Dutch sailors fleeing the monstrous spider, their faces twisted in horror as they rowed away with the sparkling gem. They had reached their ship, secreting the gem in their hold: and then they had run across the reef, tearing a hole in their ship, and the stone had been lost to the sea.

And so the spider had lived on. Day after day, year after year, a living curse had stalked the coast, feasting on each new wave of people who tried to build a seaside town, snacking on swimmers and tourists in the decades in between. Only Archie Silcock had been allowed to survive, a single companion to help the spider combat the loneliness of eternity, blissfully ignorant of the beast that shared his home.

'*What have you done?*' shrieked Max. 'I can't take us any higher!'

Anna's eyes shot open. The storm clouds were rippling above her head, crackling with a deadly glow. Sylvie was shouting something in her ear, swinging the white knife behind the carpet. Anna whirled around, her mouth falling open in terror.

The spider had grown to the size of a mountain. Its great face was hovering just beneath them, its fangs longer than goalposts, its eyes glistening like eight black moons. Max yelped as the beast swung a leg through the sky; it roared past them like a tree trunk in a hurricane, clipping the carpet with its long, hairy bristles. Sylvie and Max cried out as the carpet spiralled down to the ocean, caught in a tail-spin, their screams merging together as one.

'It's all right!' Anna tried to say. 'We're going to be okay!'

Nobody heard her. Anna took a deep breath as the carpet swooped up again, smiling at the spider as it waggled its gigantic feelers, marvelling at the incredible colours radiating from its body. Its black legs were beginning to sparkle white and silver, like the beach on a moonlit night; its dark abdomen was sprouting green and grey, like rain falling on the sandhills, or a piece of seaweed washed up by the tide. Anna hugged her friends close as the spider exploded with light, trying to reassure them that the story was almost at an end.

And then the spider slept, and its body was transformed into the ocean rocks, and the beaches, and the hills.

Lightning forked out from the clouds, cracking the sky like a mirror. It struck the spider in the centre of its monstrous body, zapping through its legs, its fangs, its eyes: but in truth, the spider's body was no longer there. A tremendous shudder passed through the earth, blasting away the wind and the rain. Anna stared down at the land in that clear, dry moment, whooping with joy, punching her fist into the quiet air.

Beneath the flying carpet was a brand new coast-line – a coastline that was smooth, not jagged, with a gentle swell lapping at a beautiful silver beach. Rows of slender sandbars stretched out to the dark waters of the reef, running through the water like long, spindly legs. The cliffs beside the stone jetty had swelled in size, bloating over the shallows like the abdomen of a great beast. Two pillars of tall black stone protruded from the jetty's end, their tips curved ever so slightly inward, dripping with the spray of the waves.

The curse of Mermaid's Purse had been lifted.

The spider was no more.

17

SKIN AND BONES

THE RAIN BLEW BACK IN AS MAX FLEW THE CARPET down to the silver beach. Anna tumbled off the carpet with an exhausted grin; Max collapsed beside her, the black cat nestled in his arms. A torn piece of dictionary was caught behind his ear; Anna pulled it free with a giggle, letting it flutter away in the breeze.

Only Sylvie didn't look comfortable sitting on

the land. She rolled quickly to the water's edge, sliding through the waves until her body was entirely submerged. With a confused blink, she sank beneath the surface, disappearing into the sea.

Max sat up suddenly.

'She's still got the knife!' he spluttered. 'She never gave it back – and now she's gone!'

Anna sighed. 'I don't think we'll be rid of her that easily,' she said. 'Just wait. She'll be back.'

She took the cat from Max and held it close, stroking its velvety black ears. The cat stared at her suspiciously, still looking rather shaken from the magic carpet ride, but after some time it closed its eyes and let its body go limp, purring like a motor as Anna patted it all over. Its blue whiskers twitched as Anna's fingers brushed against them; a tiny spark passed through Anna's skin, like a charge of static electricity.

'What *is* it, do you think?' said Max, reaching

out to stroke the cat's tail. 'I mean, it looks like a cat – but, you know.' He gave Anna a meaningful look. 'It's not a *real* cat.'

The cat opened a single eye, staring at Max through a golden slit. Max quickly withdrew his hand.

Anna didn't know what to think. They had now met the cat on three different continents – and on the past two occasions, the cat had saved their lives. It was clearly a thing of magic, but it also didn't seem to mean them any harm. Anna ran her fingers through its whiskers again, enjoying the strange tingling once more.

'Of course she's a real cat,' she said. 'She's just a long way from home, is all. A very, *very* long way.' She scratched the cat's belly. 'And if she wants to join our club, that's quite all right with me.'

The cat purred a little louder. Max rolled his eyes, falling back onto the carpet and staring up at the rippling clouds. The siblings sat in silence as the rain fell lightly upon them, enjoying the long, peaceful moment. They didn't say another word until Sylvie slithered back onto the beach beside them, her dark hair wriggling like a nest of eels.

'You've changed *everything*,' she said. Her voice wavered as she spoke, as if she couldn't quite decide whether she was upset or not. 'The rocks, and the reef, and the seabed – it's *all* different. Even the tunnels are closing themselves up.' She ran a hand over her neck. 'I only just made it there in time to gather all of these. Aren't they lovely?'

Anna shuddered. Hanging across Sylvie's breast was a new necklace – a necklace made of bones much larger than the ones that had hung there before. There were teeth and finger joints, vertebrae and ribs, all of them jangling together on a string, shining pearly white. Sylvie smiled proudly, holding up a finger to shush Max's horrified spluttering.

'Don't worry,' she said. 'I didn't take any from your *friend*. I kept her body safe. I can bring her skeleton ashore, if you like. It's just out there, hidden by the reef.'

She seemed to misunderstand why the children might find a necklace of human bones so horrible. Anna stared firmly at Sylvie's face, determined to ignore the ghastly objects dangling below.

'Thanks, Sylvie,' she said, trying to be tactful. 'That was kind of you.'

Sylvie beamed. 'I told you I'd be a good help,' she said. 'I bet I'm an excellent adventurer. I expect you'll want to ask me all kinds of questions, now that we're friends again.'

Max shot Anna a dark look. Anna knew what he was thinking. Sylvie had helped them battle the spider – but was she really as good an ally as Caspar, or Jamie, or Isabella? As far as Anna knew, none of their other friends had ever made jewellery out of human remains, and she was fairly sure they had never tried to drown anyone, either. So why did she find Sylvie so interesting? Anna ran her fingers through the cat's silky fur. Despite everything that had happened – despite the pleading look on Max's face – she still wanted to know more about the mermaid girl lying beside her. Wouldn't it be a good thing to have another friend from the fairy world?

'Here you are,' said Sylvie, as if sensing Anna's hesitance. 'I kept it safe for you. It's a strange thing for a human to have, but you are a very strange human. I think it belongs with you – for now, at least.'

She was holding out the white knife. Anna took it, relieved to feel the hilt warming her palm as usual. The heat seemed to soothe the pain the shining jewel had left behind.

'I'm sorry about the opal,' she said. 'That was your treasure, wasn't it? The one from long ago, that your sisters shared with the humans as a kindness. The mermaids told some sailors all about the stone and the spider, to try to ensure that nobody else was eaten. But then the spider kept on living, and your sisters thought the humans had betrayed them.'

'Yes,' said Sylvie. 'I was very young when it happened, but I think that's right.' She looked at Anna curiously. 'But you found it again, after all these years. How?'

Anna sighed. 'It was in the shipwreck. That's where it's been, all this time. The job you gave the sailors was too big. They fled from the spider, and then they lost the gem when their ship hit the reef.' She smiled sadly. 'But the sailors managed to send out a message. A woman named Madeleine found it in a bottle, and then she led us here too. We finally got to finish what the sailors started.'

She stared out at the sea, listening to the gentle lapping of the waves against her toes. The long, sad history of the town seemed to wash over them as they sat there, each of them thinking about how different things could have been. Nobody said anything for a very long time.

'I've got a question,' said Max eventually. He was eyeing the water nervously, still clutching the magic carpet. 'In the cave, you said you had sisters. So how many of you are there? Why have you come into our world?'

Anna thought they were very good questions. She wondered if the mermaid would give them a straight answer.

'Oh,' said Sylvie. 'I didn't think you'd want to know about *that*.' She swished her legs through the water, looking rather sad. 'I used to have many sisters — so many I could barely count them all. They carried me here long ago, through the channels where the waters bleed together, to see the oceans on the other side. It was only supposed to be a visit, I think. But the oceans were so beautiful, they decided to stay.' She paused, inhaling a deep breath of salty air. 'I was always the littlest. My sisters were sure to teach me as many things as they could, but in the end their bodies grew too old to carry on. Their skin melted away, and then their bones as well, and then they were gone. Now I'm the only one left.'

She sniffed, turning her head away from the children. Max opened his mouth and then closed it again, clearly wishing he could take his questions back. He looked at Anna for support, but Anna wasn't sure what to say either. Now Sylvie's search for a friend made perfect sense. How long had the mermaid girl been alone?

'Sorry, Sylvie,' said Max. 'I didn't know about that.'

Sylvie turned to Max kindly, her blue eyes sparkling. 'That's okay,' she said. 'I know my sisters are here somewhere. I still see them sometimes, when the light hits the water in just the right way. They smile at me, and they wave, and I know we're all together again.' She smiled brightly. 'That's why I'll never leave. I like your world. I don't need to go back to that other place. I've got everything I need right here.'

Anna's ears pricked up at the words *other place*. Sylvie was talking about the old wood – the hidden world of the fairies. She and Max had heard the place mentioned many times now, but nobody had ever told them anything about it. Would Sylvie be the one to finally divulge its secrets?

'What about the spider, then?' she said, casually shifting the cat's weight in her lap. 'Did it follow you here? Was it from the old wood too?'

Sylvie scoffed. 'The huntress didn't follow us,' she said. 'We followed *her*. She emerged from the bleed long before we did – but from the caverns, of course, not the sea.' She looked at Anna pointedly. 'She was one of the first animals, you know. In the old wood, they *all* used to be that big. That's why my sisters tried to feed her their treasure. Our stone was a piece of the wood itself – a tiny chip of foundation, taken right from the centre. They didn't mean to use it, but when they realised a huntress had escaped ...'

Anna nodded as nonchalantly as she could, but inside she felt stunned. Sylvie was talking openly about the fairy world! Words piled up in Anna's mouth as she tried to choose her next question.

'So what's it like?' she said quickly. 'The old wood. What do you remember about it? Can humans go there too?'

The cat sat upright in her lap. In an instant, sharp claws were digging into her legs; Anna opened her mouth in shock as the little cat hissed at her, revealing a sharp array of pearly white teeth.

The little cat hissed at her.

The cat placed its tiny paws on her shoulders, meeting her gaze firmly with its golden eyes. Anna had never seen an animal look so stern.

'Oh my,' said Sylvie. 'You're in trouble now. She doesn't think you're ready to know any of that.' She tilted her head. 'Maybe you don't know as much about our world as you thought?'

Anna glared at the cat. Why had it interrupted her? Wasn't it supposed to help her? As the cat nestled back into her lap, she made a point of refusing to pat it.

Sylvie giggled. 'Don't be cross. She's only doing her duty, you know. Now that she's found you, she'll protect you wherever you go. You should listen to her advice.' She smiled at the cat. 'What's her name?'

But Anna was still puzzling over what Sylvie had said. What duty did the cat have? How had it found her? She opened her mouth to ask another question, but Sylvie held up a pale finger.

'That's enough secrets for one afternoon,' she said, smirking. 'You'll only get yourself in trouble again. And besides – I can hear someone calling you. Anna. *Max.*'

Max squirmed as Sylvie said his name, but the word didn't seem to be imbued with any particular magic. Anna gave the cat a begrudging stroke, wishing Sylvie had been able to tell them more. The cat jumped lightly from her lap as she stood up, darting away into the grasses beyond the beach. Anna turned to watch it, but as the tussocks tossed back and forth, she realised she couldn't tell where it had gone.

'Don't worry,' said Sylvie. 'She'll be back.'

She reached out her hand, her fingers closing around Max's shoulder. Max spluttered as the mermaid girl pulled him into the water – but then she was hugging him close, wrapping her arms tightly around his body. Max's face was very red when she released him. He looked so funny that Anna almost laughed, but she became rather more sombre as Sylvie pulled her in for her own embrace. The bones around Sylvie's neck jangled as she held Anna close.

'Thanks for including me,' Sylvie whispered in her ear. 'I really won't forget you – bones or no bones. I promise.'

Anna hoped it was a joke. She tried not to look too alarmed as Sylvie released her, stepping away with a smile and a nod. Then they were saying their final goodbyes, and she and Max were climbing up the sandhills one last time, and Sylvie was waving a pale arm as a flicker of lightning danced across the bay, lighting the waves with an eerie glow.

Their father was waiting for them. It was time to face the music.

18

THE SPIDER'S REVENGE

THE PROFESSOR WAS WILD WITH WORRY WHEN Anna and Max finally stumbled back into their ghost town home. He scolded them furiously, lecturing them about trust and responsibility, and then he hugged them with great force, telling them how much he loved them, and how he had feared they might not come back. It was only when Anna produced Madeleine's notebook that he finally calmed down, his attention switching in an instant.

'We found it at the bottom of a rock pool,' said Anna, trying not to lie too much. 'It took us ages to fish it out. We thought it might be important, so we brought it straight to you.'

The Professor flipped reverently through the notebook, his eyes shining. He didn't seem to notice how many pages were missing. Anna had edited the book carefully on their journey home, tearing out the pages that hinted too strongly at the spider and its magic, and had dunked what was left of the book in a puddle for good measure. She smiled guiltily as the Professor hugged them once more.

'Splendid,' he said. 'Absolutely splendid. I knew there was a missing piece. This should be everything I need to tie all of Madeleine's research together.' He sat back on his heels, a sad look on his face. 'I suppose this means Madeleine isn't coming back. She could be a funny old thing, chasing tales around the world. It wasn't like her to give up on a story altogether, but I suppose, in this case, she simply must have … moved on.'

Anna looked down at her feet. Sylvie had offered to bring Madeleine's body ashore, but Anna and Max had decided that the sudden appearance of a skeleton would raise too many suspicious questions. The spider had been vanquished, but after centuries of an ancient monster preying on locals and tourists alike, the town of Mermaid's Purse was probably better off without a squadron of police poking about. Worse still, Anna suspected that Archie Silcock would have been the last person to have spoken to Madeleine, which would surely make him suspect number one if a body – or bodies – were to wash up on the shore. After everything Archie had been through, troubling him with that additional burden seemed too unfair.

And so Madeleine would stay beneath the reef,

resting peacefully among the brilliant coral. For the first time since their adventures had begun, Anna had found a missing person who needed to stay missing for good.

The Professor sighed, moving like a sleepwalker to the kitchen table, the notebook clutched in his hand. He already seemed to have forgotten about the children. Max rolled his eyes, tilting his head towards the junk room. The siblings tiptoed away, leaving the Professor to his books. Max set up the board game with the missing pieces, and the children had a marvellous time making up the rules, laughing and talking until late in the evening. As the stars came out, they slept, drifting off to the sound of falling rain.

When the children awoke the next morning, Archie Silcock was already in the living room, having a heated conversation with the Professor, who seemed very confused.

'I'm telling you, everything's different,' said Archie gruffly. 'It's not the same as it was yesterday. The hills have changed, and the paths as well. Took me hours to find the place, and two skun knees to boot.' He whirled around as Anna and Max entered the room, making the floorboards creak. 'Are the two of you to blame, then? Did you do something? Did you go out in the night?'

Anna gawped at him, too surprised to speak. Archie grimaced, tapping his walking stick against the ground.

'You've done it then,' he said. 'Only children, and you've managed to do what I never could. Curse-breakers, the lot of you.' He sighed, his body sinking down, as if a tremendous weight had been lifted from his shoulders. 'This town looked after me. I knew it was rotten, but I stayed here just the same. Couldn't shake the familiarity. Felt like I could still see the place, even with my eyes gone sour.' He sniffed. 'No good me staying here now. I don't know these hills from Adam, now you've gone and changed them. It's time I moved in with my sister for good.'

Anna nodded, feeling rather relieved. She glanced at the Professor, who was listening to Archie with a baffled expression. How could she tell Archie that his suspicions were correct?

But Archie held up a hand. He walked over to the door before she could say anything, turning the handle and stepping out into the morning light.

'No need, girl,' he said. 'I'll miss the old villain, but I'd rather not know. Take your secrets with you and be gone. I know you've got more good to do.' He grinned, showing his yellow teeth. 'It was good to meet you.'

The Professor gave a bewildered wave as Archie shuffled away, a new spring in his step, his stick tapping happily against the rocky path.

—◆—

'*The Spider's Revenge*,' said Max. 'That's a good one.'

Anna wrinkled her nose. 'It's a bit dramatic. How about, *Madeleine's Folly*?'

Max frowned. 'Mine are heaps better. *The Blind Man's Curse. The Cavern of Terror. The Great Carpet Rescue.*'

Anna looked down at the book in her lap. The emerald green journal was open to a fresh new page, glossy and white, full of possibilities. She held her fine black pen tightly as the Professor swung the car along the coastal road, thinking carefully about their latest adventure. What should it be called?

'*The Scourge of Ghost Town*,' said Max. '*Mad Max and the Daring Flight of Doom.*'

Anna flourished the pen. She wrote a new title at

the top of the page, careful not to smudge the ink as the car bumped down the road. She smiled in satisfaction, showing the page to Max.

THE MERMAID WRECK.

Max wrinkled his nose. 'That's no good. You don't even mention the spider, *or* my flying carpet.'

'That's because they're surprises,' said Anna. 'We don't want the others to know exactly what's coming.' She grinned. 'I bet Isabella and Jamie will hate this one. I don't think either of them like spiders.'

'Caspar will like it, though,' said Max, shuddering. 'He loves creepy-crawlies.'

Anna smiled. Australia had tested them like never before – but with the adventure complete, the story needed to be recorded. Soon the pages of the emerald journal would be filled with a new tale, of a blighted town, and a lonely beast, and the thrilling events that put an end to the curse, once and for all.

'Final offer,' said Max. '*The Day We Almost Gave Dad a Heart Attack.*'

Anna snorted. She glanced at the Professor in the rear-view mirror, feeling pleased as she caught a glimpse of his face. On her walk to meet Sylvie on the beach, she had thought of herself as being like Madeleine Graves, filled with boundless curiosity – but, of course, she hadn't inherited that from Madeleine at all. It was the Professor who had given her a love of stories, and of adventures, and of seeking answers wherever they might be. Where did he plan on taking them next?

Max dug his fingers into the gap beside his seat, crowing in delight as he pulled out an old lolly bag. Anna grinned, scribbling some notes on the side of the page, wincing as a strange pain tingled down her fingers. Touching the white knife had soothed her palm, but she could still feel the welt the shining stone had left behind. The pain excited her. For just a few hours, she had held a piece of the old wood itself — a chip of pure magic, burning all the way to her bones. Somewhere out there — in this world or another — was a whole *land* of magic, filled with monsters and mermaids and mysterious cats. Would she ever succeed in seeing it herself?

Max's eyes had already drooped closed, a lolly snake hanging limply from his mouth. Anna frowned, flexing her fingers, marvelling at the strange new shine to her skin. She liked magic very much — but so far, nobody was prepared to show her where to get any more of it. That didn't seem fair at all. Why should the monsters have all the fun?

Next time, things would be different. If the fairies came to endanger her life once again, Anna was determined not to finish the adventure without claiming another treasure. A spell, perhaps. Or a potion. Or a wand.

She laughed to herself as the car sped away, her eyes shining very, very bright.

THE END

BOOK ONE
THE VAMPIRE KNIFE

A storm is raging around the forests of Transylvania, where siblings Anna and Max are visiting with the Professor. Something evil is lurking in the trees — and it seems to have a taste for human blood.

When Max goes missing, it's up to Anna and her new friend Isabella to find him. But even if they can rescue him, Max will never be the same again ...

BE BOLD. BE BRAVE. BE TERRIFIED.

BOOK TWO
THE TROLL HEART

When Anna, Max and the Professor arrive in the foggy fields of England, they stumble into a mystery: a boy has vanished near a strange river, lost without a trace.

Armed with her magical white knife, Anna is convinced that another monster is involved. But when the sinister secret of the river is finally revealed, will she and Max be able to save the missing boy – and themselves?

PAY THE TOLL. BLOOD OR GOLD.

BOOK THREE
THE GENIE RINGS

A vast citadel of sand and stone, built long ago by a great sorceress, has been unearthed in the Iranian desert. The Professor is searching the ruin for the ending to an ancient fairy story – but for Anna and Max, a dangerous new tale is beginning.

A sinister figure is trying to find the lost treasure of the sorceress – which might be a fairy weapon. Anna and Max must ensure it stays hidden, or else a monster of epic proportions could be unleashed …

BE CAREFUL WHAT YOU WISH FOR.

DO YOU DARE TO READ ALL OF THE WITCHING HOURS?

COMING SOON: BOOK 6
THE GIANT KEY

ACKNOWLEDGEMENTS

It took four whole books for Anna and Max to finally make it to my home country. In the lead up to their arrival, I spent a very long time plotting and scheming, all to make sure the children's visit to Australia would be their scariest adventure yet. Thank you to everyone who supported me during the writing of this dark, twisted book: for posterity, your names have been recorded below.

As always, the wickedest supporters of all were the good witches of Hardie Grant Egmont, who were more than happy to send Anna and Max into a spider's lair; I am forever grateful for the supernatural patience of Marisa, Luna, Penelope, Haylee, Ella, Pooja, Kristy, Emily, Tye, Joanna, Madeleine, Julia and Annabel. Further thanks go to Alison Arnold, an honorary witch who worked some extra magic at the eleventh hour.

Master of illustrations Ryan Andrews has returned from the deep to draw some of the scariest mermaids ever recorded: once again, I thank him for his courage. Lise Wouters translated the Dutch, and also helped me invent a name for the very spooky shipwreck. *Hartelijk bedankt!*

I've never liked the beach, but my friends Ellen and Sophie (and Jemima) were kind enough to drive me to a deserted stretch of coastline on a stormy day, and were patient with me while I climbed over slippery rocks and got myself thoroughly soaked. It was lovely of you to help me, and I'm sorry that we ruined Sophie's beautiful coat.

Finally, thank you to my cat, Teddy (my number one writing assistant), and also to the enormous huntsman spider that bit me on the finger last May, in the very middle of the night. Blood was literally spilled during the writing of this story, and I think the book is all the better for it.

ABOUT THE AUTHOR

JACK HENSELEIT was born on a winter evening in 1991, just after the stroke of midnight. When the weather is dark and stormy, he writes fairy tales – *real* fairy tales, where witches and goblins play tricks on unwary girls and boys. Not all of the tales have happy endings.

The Mermaid Wreck is his fourth novel. Visit jackhenseleit.com to learn more about Jack.